Tales of Sex and Violence

Wendy Doniger O'Flaherty

Tales of Sex and Violence

Folklore, Sacrifice, and Danger in the *Jaiminīya Brāhmaṇa*

The University of Chicago Press
Chicago and London

Wendy Doniger O'Flaherty is professor of History of Religions and Indian Studies in the Divinity School, the Department of South Asian Languages and Civilizations, the Committee on Social Thought, and the College at the University of Chicago. Among her previous publications are *Asceticism and Eroticism in the Mythology of Śiva*; *Hindu Myths: A Sourcebook Translated from the Sanskrit*; *The Origins of Evil in Hindu Mythology*; *The Rig Veda: An Anthology*; *Women, Androgynes, and Other Mythical Beasts*; and *Dreams, Illusion, and Other Realities*.

The University of Chicago Press, Chicago 60637
The University of Chicago Press, Ltd., London

Printed in the United States of America
94 93 92 91 90 89 88 87 86 85 54321

Library of Congress Cataloging Publication Data

O'Flaherty, Wendy Doniger.
Tales of sex and violence.

Includes original translations of 27 tales.
Bibliography: p.
Includes index.
1. Brāhmaṇas. *Jaiminīya Brāhmaṇa*—Criticism, interpretation, etc. 2. Folklore—India. 3. India—Social life and customs. I. Brāhmaṇas. *Jaiminīya Brāhmaṇa*. English. Selections. 1985. II. Title.
BL1121.3.J356034 1985 294.5'921 84-16393

ISBN 0-226-61852-8

This book is for my son, Michael,
who listened to my Indian stories when he was young,
and told me so many of his own as he grew up

and for my friend Sudhir Kakar,
who helped me to understand dreams

Contents

List of Abbreviations

AB	*Aitareya Brāhmaṇa*
AV	*Atharva Veda*
BAU	*Bṛhadāraṇyaka Upaniṣad*
BŚS	*Baudhāyana Śrauta Sūtra*
GB	*Gopatha Brāhmaṇa*
JAOS	*Journal of the American Oriental Society*
JB	*Jaiminīya Brāhmaṇa*
JUB	*Jaiminīya Upaniṣad Brāhmaṇa*
KāṭhB	*Kāṭhaka Brāhmaṇa*
KB	*Kauṣītaki Brāhmaṇa*
Ku	*Kaṭha Upaniṣad*
MBh	*Mahābhārata*
MS	*Maitrāyaṇī Saṃhitā*
PB	*Pañcaviṃśa Brāhmaṇa*
ṚV	*Ṛg Veda*
ŚB	*Śāṭyāyana Brāhmaṇa*
ṢB	*Ṣaḍviṃśa Brāhmaṇa*
ŚKhB	*Śankhāyana Brāhmaṇa*
ŚPB	*Śatapatha Brāhmaṇa*
SV	*Sāma Veda*
TB	*Taittirīya Brāhmaṇa*
TS	*Taittirīya Saṃhitā*
VS	*Vājasaneyī Saṃhitā*
YV	*Yajur Veda*
Lost Brāhmaṇas.	See note at end of bibliography of Sanskrit texts.

Acknowledgments

This book was begun during a year, 1981, when a grant from the John Simon Guggenheim Memorial Foundation not only relieved me of my academic responsibilities but, by giving me time to read Sanskrit texts and books about dreams and about folklore, inspired me to write a book about the *Jaiminīya Brāhmaṇa*. I am also grateful to Dean Franklin Gamwell of the University of Chicago Divinity School, who helped me to arrange my subsequent teaching commitments in such a way that it was possible to make the best use of the Guggenheim, and who reassured me, when I doubted it, that my way of self-education is through writing, not through reading alone.

Among the colleagues whose advice and encouragement are reflected in this book, I would like to express my special gratitude to Brian K. Smith, who read the Brāhmaṇas with me, picked up many of my biases and converted me to some of his own, found and copied the translations and articles that I needed, and, finally, read the manuscript, wisely and enthusiastically. Herman Tull kindly shared with me his vintage collection of European scholars' scornful assessments of the Brāhmaṇas. David Szanton of the Joint Committee on South Asia of the Social Science Research Council and the American Council of Learned Societies goaded me on and added fuel to my fires by sending me to the conference on folklore held in Mysore in August, 1980, under the auspices of the S.S.R.C. David Grene, David Knipe, David Shulman, Jan Heesterman, Stuart Blackburn, and Sudhir Kakar read an early draft carefully and generously. I owe a great deal to the students who read the *Jaiminīya Brāhmaṇa* with me: Barry Friedman, Charles S. Hallisey, Gail Hinich, David Carpenter, William K. Mahony, Bruce Sullivan, David Lawrence, and David White, as well as Brian K. Smith and Herman Tull. I am grateful to Alan Dundes for supplying an elusive Stith Thompson motif, and I am indebted to Douglas Sell for helping me to make the index. The jacket photograph, of a mysterious *pietà* involving a god of death, a goddess of fertility, and a dead young man, was taken by Carmel Berkson, who made a special trip to Ellora with me in order to photograph it. A. K. Ramanujan not only taught me most of what I know about Indian folklore, but helped me to talk through the book during many Hyde Park conversations at twilight.

Tales of Sex and Violence

1
Introduction: Folklore and Dreams in 900 B.C.

The Western Scorn for the Brāhmaṇas

I have loved the *Jaiminīya Brāhmaṇa* (henceforth *Jaiminīya*) ever since I stumbled on it some twenty years ago. Stumbled indeed, since it could hardly be called a widely praised or highly recommended work; on the contrary, my affection for it could be regarded as idiosyncratic at best, perverse at worst, and certainly contrary. The great American Indologist W. D. Whitney wrote of it, five years after its existence was made known to Western scholarship almost exactly a century ago:

> The *Jaiminīya* is on the whole a dull and uninteresting work, as compared with others of its class. A most unreasonable share of its immense mass is taken up with telling on what occasion some being "saw" a particular *sāman* [chant] and "praised with it," thereby attaining certain desired ends, which may be attained by others that will follow his example, and the *pseudo*-legends thus reported or fabricated average of a degree of flatness and artificiality quite below the ordinary. [Whitney 1883, pp. viii–ix]

Apparently Whitney's belief (obscured by the awkward grammar, which we may take to be an expression of his impatience with the text he is discussing) was that the *Jaiminīya* was even *more* "flat and artificial" than the other Brāhmaṇas. What, then, was the standard set by the other Brāhmaṇas, the standard that the *Jaiminīya* failed to attain? By far the most famous of the Brāhmaṇas, then as now, was the *Śatapatha*, a mammoth text, translated by Julius Eggeling and published in 1882 after close to a lifetime of hard work on five heavy volumes. What was the inspiration that sustained Eggeling in this great task? Surely not admiration for the text itself, for poor old Eggeling began his introduction to the translation with the following desperate and rather peevish complaint:

> The translator of the *Śatapatha-brāhmaṇa* can be under no illusion as to the reception his production is likely to meet with at the hand of the general reader. In the whole range of literature few works are probably less calculated to excite the interest of any outside the very limited number of specialists, than the ancient theological writings of the Hindus, known by the name of Brāhmaṇas. For wearisome prolixity of exposition, characterised by dogmatic assertion and a flimsy symbolism rather than by serious reasoning, these works are perhaps not equalled anywhere; unless, indeed, it be by the speculative vapourings of the Gnostics, than which, in the opinion of the learned translators of Irenaeus, "nothing more absurd has probably ever been imagined by rational beings." [Eggeling 1882, p. ix]

Eggeling's opinion was shared by the greatest Vedic scholar of that first generation, the man who published the first European edition of the *Ṛg Veda* and who founded the Sacred Books of the East series in which Eggeling's translation was published: Friedrich Max Müller. Twenty years before Eggeling brought out his translation, Max Müller called the Brāhmaṇas

> a literature which for pedantry and downright absurdity can hardly be matched anywhere. . . . The general character of these works is marked by shallow and insipid grandiloquence, by priestly conceit, and antiquarian pedantry. . . . These works deserve to be studied as the

> physician studies the twaddle of idiots, and the raving of madmen. [Müller 1860, p. 389]

This passage begins with a phrase ("can hardly be matched anywhere") that was later picked up by Eggeling; it also contains a concept that was to be swallowed whole by Indologists for generations to come: the belief that the Brāhmaṇas represented a period of mental degeneration in India ("the raving of madmen"). Another term, "twaddle," is one that Müller himself became rather fond of and reused on several later occasions—even forty years later:

> However interesting the Brāhmaṇas may be to students of Indian literature, they are of small interest to the general reader. The greater portion of them is simply twaddle, and what is worse, theological twaddle. No person who is not acquainted beforehand with the place which the Brāhmaṇas fill in the history of the Indian mind, could read more than ten pages without being disgusted. . . . Such books, which no circulating library would touch, [represent] a most important phase in the growth of the human mind, in its passage from health to disease. [Müller 1900, pp. 113–14]

In this same year, Arthur A. Macdonell (who had the Boden Professorship at Oxford that Max Müller had hoped to win) borrowed the old "can hardly be matched anywhere" construction as applied to the Brāhmaṇas, which, he said, "form an aggregate of shallow and pedantic discussions, full of sacerdotal conceits, and fanciful, or even absurd, identifications, such as is doubtless unparalleled anywhere else" (Macdonell 1900, p. 32).

Neither the Indologists' opinion of the Brāhmaṇas nor their tendency to parrot one another's terms of abuse improved on continued acquaintance. What "twaddle" was to Max Müller, "inanity" was to Whitney, who referred to the Brāhmaṇas as "in general tediously discursive, verbose, and artificial, and in no small part absolutely puerile and inane" (Whitney 1873, p. 68); a decade later, he had more of the same to say of the Brāhmaṇas,

> whereof the excessive and puzzling intricacy, the minuteness and triviality of details, with the general inanity of their exposition and justification, are beyond belief. We have here one of the aberrations of the human mind. . . . Their tedious inanity . . . will soon satiate, if it does not disgust, the general reader. [Whitney 1882, pp. 392–93]

The theme of the decay of the human mind is a legacy from Müller; and Whitney's "puerile inanity" was in turn bequeathed to Charles Lanman, who referred to the Brāhmaṇas as "puerile, arid, inane" (Lanman 1884, p. 357). This "inanity" was reflected above all in the stories told in the Brāhmaṇas, texts that Whitney took to task for "their misapprehensions and deliberate perversions of their text, their ready invention of tasteless and absurd legends to explain the allusions, real or fancied, which it contains, their often atrocious etymologies" (Whitney 1873, p. 110).

This condemnation suggests as least one reason why the *Jaiminīya* was at first dismissed even more disdainfully than were the other Brāhmaṇas: if the stories are the most worthless part of the generally worthless Brāhmaṇas, then a Brāhmaṇa like the *Jaiminīya*, which has the most, and most fully treated, stories, is the most worthless of all. Yet this opinion of the text did not persist indefinitely, as we will see when we turn now to the history of the publication of the *Jaiminīya*.

The History of the *Jaiminīya Brāhmaṇa* in the West

In 1878, A. C. Burnell published (in a limited edition of fifty copies) the *Jaiminīya* version of "Bhṛgu's Journey in the Other World" (*JB* 1. 42–44). This publication (Burnell 1878) was noted by Whitney in a brief communication to the American Oriental Society in 1883 (the occasion for the remark by Whitney with which I began this discussion), in which Whitney translated the *Jaiminīya* tale "The Rejuvenation of Cyavana" (*JB* 3. 120–29). After that, the work of editing, publishing, and translating the *Jaiminīya* fell to two other scholars, W. Caland and Hanns Oertel, both of whom were interested first and foremost in its folk literature.

Oertel began by publishing a series of extracts from the *Jaiminīya Brāhmaṇa* and from the closely related *Jaiminīya Upaniṣad Brāhmaṇa*, beginning in 1893 in volume 15 of the *Journal of the American Oriental Society* and continuing (mostly in that journal, but occasionally elsewhere, once in Connecticut, once in Paris, once in Germany) through 1909. Oertel's selection dealt, almost without exception, with narratives. His work at Yale was conveniently supported by that of his younger colleague, E. W. Hopkins, who published, in 1909, excerpts from the *Pañcaviṃśa Brāhmaṇa* (also called the *Tāṇḍya-Mahā-Brāhmaṇa*); he, too, selected the folk narratives, and he noted the parallels with the *Jaiminīya Brāhmaṇa*. The work of editing the *Jaiminīya*, publishing a book of selected translations (into German), and translating the entire *Pañcaviṃśa* (into English) was done by W. Caland, who first published an introduction to the *Jaiminīya* in 1907 and then, in 1919, published a volume of selected texts (which he himself had edited), together with German translations. Then, in his 1931 English translation of the *Pañcaviṃśa*, Caland appended to many of the stories his English translations of the *Jaiminīya* parallels, criticizing Oertel's translations *en passant* and referring the reader to the German translations he had published in 1919. It was not until 1954 that a complete Sanskrit text of the *Jaiminīya Brāhmaṇa* was published (by Raghu Vira and Lokesh Chandra), an edition that improved upon many of the readings of Oertel and Caland.

A number of factors contributed to this desultory European response to the text of the *Jaiminīya*. The emphasis in Vedic studies at this time was on sacrifice, an emphasis that was enhanced by the great success of the work of Henri Hubert and Marcel Mauss. This work, published at the end of the nineteenth century, has enjoyed a renaissance in our own generation through the influence of Madeleine Biardeau, Charles Malamoud, and other Indologists of the French school. Thus, scholarly attention has been focused all along on the sacrificial formulae of the Brāhmaṇas, and these are truly difficult to appreciate, for their elegance is obscured by a terminology and web of cultural assumptions that continue to elude most scholars.

The *Jaiminīya*, however, had been known from the first as, primarily, a book of stories; the first excerpts published from it were stories, including several of those that appear in the present work. At first this characterization tended to obscure the importance of the *Jaiminīya*; for scholars of that period, certain that the Brāhmaṇas were about the sacrifice and that the stories in the Brāhmaṇas were not about the sacrifice, regarded the stories as irrelevant interpolations. Yet the very fact that the texts selected from the *Jaiminīya* for publication were stories rather than ritual passages suggests that a change in emphasis had begun to take place; it indicates the dawning realization that the Brāhmaṇa stories were interesting after all and that the neglected *Jaiminīya*, which has the most interesting stories, might perhaps be one of the most interesting of the Brāhmaṇas. Thus, when all the other Brāhmaṇas were still being condemned for pedantry and shallowness, some scholars began to argue that the *Jaiminīya* stories had a separate value of their own.

This about-face with regard to the appreciation of the *Jaiminīya Brāhmaṇa* resulted from the increasing influence that the growing science of folklore was having on Vedic philologists. It is surely no coincidence that the articles on the *Jaiminīya* that Oertel published in the 1890s came at a time when Europe was beginning to discover the German *Märchen* and the Finnish Epics; several of Oertel's articles are devoted to European parallels to the Indian texts (or rather, as the ethnocentric European Indologists of the time put it, to Indian parallels to well-known European tales). While Max Müller was trying to make the Hindoos respectable by dredging up links between the *Ṛg Veda* and Homer, Oertel was finding links on a much "lower" level of society.

Why did Oertel's work have so little impact on subsequent treatments of Indian folklore and literature, let alone world folklore? There were several reasons. Oertel published his text in a highly respectable but rather elite Orientalist journal; Caland's book was never translated into English; none of these works was likely to find its way into Stith Thompson's index of folk motifs. But more important, I think, was the genre of the stories, whose flavor was not to European tastes. These stories were often quite obscene; Oertel lapsed into a blushing (and extremely poor) Latin when he encountered particularly "frank" bits, and he even fled to a Parisian journal to publish his essay on the dirtiest story of all, the tale of "Long-Tongue the Demoness" (*JB* 1. 161–63). Whitney discussed this same story only in order to tabulate the occurrence of perfect and imperfect verbs in it, and even then he used the *Pañcaviṃśa* version of the tale, merely noting that "the same story is told, at much greater length and in less decent fashion," in the *Jaiminīya* (Whitney 1892, p. 7). Nineteenth-century Indologists were interested in the genders of words, not the genders of demons.

Even when the stories were published, no one seemed to know what to make of their banal detail, their slang-ridden conversations, their physical violence, their obsession with the same family relationships, described over and over again. No one tried to discern patterns, or to distill attitudes, from the tales; no one tried to place them in a cultural context. Without these ways of making sense of the corpus—ways that had to await the era of Propp and Freud and Frazer—one could not do much but translate them and point out similar stories in Pausanias and Hesiod. One could not really make much *sense* out of them, and so they continued to be classified as nonsense.

Folklore in the *Jaiminīya Brāhmaṇa*

Since Whitney's first attack on the *Jaiminīya*, a hundred years ago, the science of folklore has revolutionized our attitudes toward texts such as these. Now we recognize the importance of folklore and no longer regard it as the poor cousin of mythology. Indeed, many people feel that it is useless to separate the two at all. The dichotomy took hold in European circles when British classicists and anthropologists, under the influence of Jane Ellen Harrison and Lord Raglan, explored the hypothesis that myths and rituals are inevitably linked; folktales, by contrast, were not expected to have any connection with ritual. Now, the Brāhmaṇas are Sanskrit texts composed around 900 B.C. by priests in order to explain the meaning and purpose of the Vedic ritual. That is their ostensible and ever-present agenda; every line is permeated with explicit references to the Vedic sacrifice. That being so, one assumed that the stories they told must be myths, not folktales; it followed, then, that any stories in the Brāhmaṇas that were *not* about the sacrifice, and therefore were not myths, were worthless interpolations.

The flaws in this argument result from the false distinction between myth and folktale, the false corollary distinction between the Great and the Little Tradition, and the false assumption that myth is always associated with ritual. Let us look at these problems one by one. It is increasingly apparent that it is misleading to use the terms myth and folktale to distinguish two discrete genres. As Ananda K. Coomaraswamy put it, "The content of folklore is metaphysical" (Coomaraswamy 1956, p. 136). The most one could hope to do would be to postulate a kind of continuum, with stories located all along the line, some more "folk" than "myth," some the reverse. But, even to do this, one would have to associate "folk" with tales that deal primarily with human problems, often in a profane context and usually with primarily human protagonists and a minimal intervention of the supernatural, while "myth" would deal primarily with cosmic problems, in a sacred context and with supernatural actors. I have found it useful to distinguish between stories with these two different emphases in the *Jaiminīya*, but I do not think it wise to say that the stories that I have called folktales are not myths. They are myths with a particularly worldly, human, nonsupernatural bent, perhaps even a nonreligious bent (which is why it is at first surprising to find them in a text devoted to a ritual); they are stories about families and about the problems posed for us by the human body. And since they often appear side by side *in the same text* (in this case, the *Jaiminīya*) with more cosmic, theological stories, it becomes increasingly problematic to regard them as a genre distinct from mythology.

The idea of the Great and the Little Tradition, which spawned so many fresh insights, has now begun to exert a drag backwards on the first impetus that it set in motion. In India, in particular, such works as Srinivas's studies of Sanskritization (and the inverse, localization), together with Louis Dumont's analyses of the anthropology of classical Indian civilization, David Shulman's work on Tamil and Sanskrit mythology, and McKim Marriott's studies of pan-Indian (contemporary and classical) cognitive categories, have erased once and for all the line dividing the Brahmins from the folk. More recently, A. K. Ramanujan has pointed out the "permeable membranes" that demarcate not only structure and antistructure in India but, within this division, the Great and the Little Tradition and their further subdivisions (Ramanujan 1973, p. 34).

If it can be established (as I think it can) that the Brāhmaṇas, so long accused of being the private property of the most elite and obfuscating textualists who ever lived, are in fact the vehicle for a great deal of material virtually indistinguishable in tone and plot from the stories collected by the Brothers Grimm in German farmhouses, how can one possibly separate the "folk" material from the "classical" material? One can always say, of course, that they form two entirely discrete bodies of culture that have somehow been fused in this particular text. But if they were already fused by 900 B.C., how useful is it to go on separating them into two different piles for the rest of Indo-European history? Yet, since the stories in the *Jaiminīya* were written in Sanskrit, and written by priests, they have been identified as part of the "Great Tradition." It is strange that this prejudice persists when we know how much folk material there is in later Sanskrit works, such as the *Hitopadeśa* and the *Pañcatantra* (not to mention the Pali Buddhist *Jātaka* stories). But the *Hitopadeśa* and the *Pañcatantra* are regarded as folklore because they are secular; the sacred Brāhmaṇas, it has been assumed, could not descend to the level of mere *Märchen*, plunging bathetically from myth into folktale.

Hanns Oertel, in his analysis of the story of "Long-Tongue the Dcmoness" (Oertel 1897; *JB* 1. 161–63), suggests a formulation of the competing concerns of sacrificial ritual and folk narrative in the Brāhmaṇas, with special reference to the *Jaiminīya*. He divides the texts of this particular story (although his remarks are clearly applicable to other Brāhmaṇa stories, too) into two groups, the first represented by the *Aitareya Brāhmaṇa, Maitrāyaṇī Saṃhitā*, and *Kāṭhaka Brāhmaṇa*, the second by the *Jaiminīya* and the *Pañcaviṃśa*. The first group introduces the story of Long-Tongue in order to explain why the oblation of curds has its peculiar form; the second group does not connect Long-Tongue with the oblation. Oertel deduces from this that the second group (the *Jaiminīya* and *Pañcaviṃśa*) "undoubtedly give the story in its original form" (ibid., p. 233), and he goes on to argue that this group uses this and other legends for "purely illustrative purposes. . . . Their mythological value lies in this complete absence of a motive for tampering with the received version. And there is little ground to fear, that an overpowering imagination led the Brāhmaṇical writers to poetical expansions" (ibid., p. 235). This is a rather weak argument, further weakened by Oertel's inability to resist taking a passing swipe at the absurd unlikelihood of any "overpowering imagination" on the part of the author of our text. He argues that, since the story is not intended to explain some peculiarity of the ritual, there was no need to construct it to fit the needs of the moment. Instead, he implies that it was drawn from "popular" materials (since the *Jaiminīya* author lacked the imagination to make up a story all by himself). Moreover, the Brahmins did not "tamper" with it in subsequent years, since they had no ritual axes to grind; the story did not *matter*, since it did not explain the ritual.

Why was the story told at all? "Legends of this class are solely intended to restore details omitted in a [Ṛg Vedic text], to furnish material for understanding an allusion, to explain (as in our case here [the tale of Long-Tongue]), the special circumstances under which a certain *ṛṣi* saw a hymn which bears his name, etc." (ibid., p. 235). These are the *excuses* for the tale, I agree; but I would question the assumption that they are the *reasons* or true motivations for the telling of the stories in the peculiar forms they assume in the *Jaiminīya*. How do the tales of this class of Brāhmaṇas (the *Jaiminīya* and the *Pañcaviṃśa*) differ from those in Oertel's first class, the ones that use the tale of Long-Tongue to explain the form of the oblation of curds? These latter tell their legends "*not* for the sake of the *legend as a whole*, but on account of *certain items* in it by which a given part of the ritual may be explained . . . , using a legend which in its popular form contained *some* of the facts he needs, while by *alterations and additions of his own* he makes it completely suitable for his purpose. . . . Hence the barrenness of many of these stories" (ibid., p. 236). Again he knocks the Brāhmaṇas, but this time he is on stronger grounds: the author of the text of this type (not the *Jaiminīya* type) ruins a good story by manipulating it for his sacerdotal ends. This is the "motive for tampering" with the popular tale in the first place, and now it becomes a motive for tampering with it again, at a later stage, in order to make it fit a subsequently altered form of the ritual.

Thus, Oertel concludes, "Whenever two versions of the same legend are found, . . . that version should be regarded as nearest to the popular form which is *not* connected with any ritualistic exegesis" (ibid., p. 236). Here I agree with Oertel. When the *Jaiminīya* supplies a long folktale, self-contained and consistent in its details, in place of a short phrase that occurs in another text (or, more rarely, in place of a long tale turning on a point of ritual), the *Jaiminīya* is almost certainly telling a story that had been in the air in India for a long time.

This is *not* to say that the *Jaiminīya* text is older than the text containing the ritual phrase or the ritual story, for it would have been easy enough for the *Jaiminīya* author, working from a ritual phrase or story, simply to embroider it with a long folktale. Nor is it to say that the *Jaiminīya* author just picked up a folktale and stuck it in (as Oertel seems to imply, both in his final argument and in his scornful disavowal of the possibility that the author might have used his imagination). It is simply to say that the story told in the *Jaiminīya* is probably a very old story. It is of course, at the very least, as old as the *Jaiminīya*—c. 900 B.C.—and one wonders how much profit there is in arguing about whether it is, in addition, older than other texts of the same genre and general period.

Caland argues that, where the *Jaiminīya* tells in full a story that the *Pañcaviṃśa* tells only briefly, the *Jaiminīya* is the older text, to which the *Pañcaviṃśa* gives a cryptic reference (Caland 1931, p. xix). This implies that the author of the *Pañcaviṃśa* knew, and assumed that his audience knew, the *Jaiminīya* story—an assumption that is supported by the fact that the *Pañcaviṃśa* and *Ṣaḍviṃśa* are, together with the *Jaiminīya*, the three Brāhmaṇas attached as commentaries to the same one of the three Vedas, the *Sāma Veda*, and were probably composed within the same tradition. Indeed, the impression one gets of the priests who devoted themselves to the Brāhmaṇas (each school fastidiously memorizing its own Vedic text and commentaries), is somewhat reminiscent of the group of intellectuals at the end of Ray Bradbury's *Fahrenheit 451*, who wander about, each one muttering to himself the classic text that he alone memorized when all the books in the world were burnt. The relative autonomy of the Vedic schools also accounts for the fact that the other Brāhmaṇas of the *Sāma Veda* (the *Pañcaviṃśa* and the *Ṣaḍviṃśa*, together with the reconstructed fragments of the *Śātyāyaṇa*) supply most of the close parallels to the *Jaiminīya*. It is also worth noting, as Frits Staal has suggested to me, that everything in the *Sāma Veda* is longer than its counterparts in the other Vedas; each chant is drawn out, repeated, sung on various tones, so that a single syllable may occupy several minutes of intricate cadenzas. This being so, it is hardly surprising that the stories in a *Sāma Veda* Brāhmaṇa such as the *Jaiminīya* are longer and more rococo than their counterparts in the Brāhmaṇas of other Vedas, though it does not explain why the *Jaiminīya* is more elaborate than the other *Sāma Veda* Brāhmaṇas.

One could, of course, argue the other way: that the *Jaiminīya* expanded the *Pañcaviṃśa* text. Although this argument may be less convincing, since it fails to account for the elliptic nature of the *Pañcaviṃśa* (laziness? thrift?), there is sufficient precedent for this sort of ellipsis in the *Ṛg Veda* itself to make the two arguments balance out pretty evenly. In any case, what is significant is the fact that the *Jaiminīya*, and only the *Jaiminīya*, drew on a folk source—a fact that we know, not from juggling the Indian variants, but by having recourse to our knowledge of other forms of the same story in the folk literatures of the world. Whether the *Jaiminīya* added that folk material to an extant *Pañcaviṃsa* text, or the *Pañcaviṃśa* omitted it when citing an extant *Jaiminīya* text, is of secondary interest to us. The real question is why the *Jaiminīya* used this material when the *Pañcaviṃśa* did not. For the *Jaiminīya* is quite different in its style and emphases from the other *Sāma Veda* Brāhmaṇas. Whether this individuality represents the idiosyncrasies of a single author or of a school is perhaps impossible to determine with certainty, but that there is something recognizable about the *Jaiminīya*'s way of telling stories is, I think, a defensible hypothesis, and I will try to defend it.

Sacrifice and Danger in the *Jaiminīya Brāhmaṇa*

In selecting the stories to tell in this book, I have deliberately ignored the portions of the *Jaiminīya* that deal explicitly with what is traditionally called myth or the Great Tradition. The cosmic stories of the gods and demons, the killing of the serpent Vṛtra, the creation of the world, the origin of death, the winning of immortality—all of these are the normal, central concerns of the Brāhmaṇas; all of them are well known, well understood, and well distributed through all the Brāhmaṇas, including the *Jaiminīya*. I have omitted them in order to present in a concentrated form the *other* side of the *Jaiminīya*: its idiosyncratic and apparently profane concerns. Yet, though many of these stories do not seem to be about the sacrifice, they are tied, however indirectly, to the central theme of the Brāhmaṇas, thus belying the claim that the stories are irrelevant or at least peripheral to the texts in which they occur. For the stories are about the sacrifice, after all: they are about certain shadows of the sacrifice that are obscured in the rituals but are illuminated by the narratives.

In 900 B.C., if you composed a Sanskrit treatise (or, rather, if you wanted to compose one that would be memorized and preserved), there was only one form that you could use: you composed a Brāhmaṇa based on the sacrificial tradition of the school into which you were born and/or initiated. The sacrifice already had a certain number of myths associated with it, as is clear from the tantalizing allusions in the *Ṛg Veda*, but it probably did not have a systematized mythology, let alone a systematized folklore. What mythology there was appears in the *Jaiminīya* in the form of stories that are shared, in more or less the same form, with other Brāhmaṇas: the "grand" tales of the victory of the gods over the demons, the finding of the sun, and so forth. But the *Jaiminīya* also tells many long folktales that are not found elsewhere in the Brāhmaṇas or that are found elsewhere only in a much reduced form. These stories, many of which do not have any antecedents in the milieu that we can extrapolate from the *Ṛg Veda*, are evidently not essential to the explanation of the ritual, since the ritual is explained in other texts without recourse to these stories. Moreover, if it can be demonstrated (and I think it can, by recourse to the Antti Aarne–Stith Thompson Index, at the very least) that these stories, or others much like them, also appear in other cultures, entirely divorced from any possible connection with Vedic ritual, then one can, I think, conclude that the ritual is not the only key to the meaning of the stories.

Yet these stories must have had *some* meaning related to the ritual, since they became assimilated to the basic cognitive system of the ancient Indian Brahmin ritualism of the *Jaiminīya*. And in fact, when we look more closely at the stories, we find that they are all connected to the sacrifice on the very deepest level. Since the sacrifice was the focal point for all forms of creative expression during the period of the Brāhmaṇas, texts purporting to gloss the sacrifice attracted to themselves not only material necessary for the elucidation of the sacrifice but everything else that could be dragged in to express the meaning of life in ancient India, whether or not it had any obvious bearing on the particular ritual point being glossed. To state it somewhat differently: since the sacrifice was believed to symbolize everything that was meaningful in human life, *any* compelling insight into that life would eventually gravitate to the traditional literature that was constantly coalescing about the sacrifice.

Yet the authors of the Brāhmaṇas—and, in particular, the author(s) of the *Jaiminīya*—do not bring *everything* into the text; they tend to bring a certain sort of thing into the text. The *Jaiminīya* attracts to itself images of death, sex, and the human body; more particularly, it attracts images that express the dangers inherent in death, sex, and the human body. These images are embedded in narratives about sacrifice, and they slip easily into place in such narratives, since the sacrifice itself is about death, sex, and the human body. Its elemental components (fire, water) and actions (killing, copulating) provide an arena in which the author of the *Jaiminīya* could dramatize certain insights that are also expressed in the folklore on which he drew.

The fact that the wild stories of the *Jaiminīya* are set in the midst of a tame sacerdotal formula is a clue to the process of their genesis—or, rather, to their transformation from folklore into liturgy. The *Jaiminīya* seems to me in places to be a kind of free-association oral composition, almost as if someone had said to the author, "Tell me a story about blood and butter, any story you like, the first story that comes to mind." If he returns again and again to certain themes that are not determined by the sacrificial context, we might regard that context as a kind of Rohrschach into which he projects his own subconscious concerns. But the arbitrariness of the sacrificial symbolism is perched, it must be emphasized, on the tip of an enormous heap of culturally determined scraps, and it is from these that the ritualist selects the elements of his personal *bricolage*. After chanting the Vedic texts for years and years, the author(s) must have found that certain parts of the ritual had special meanings that sparked off bursts of vivid narrative; chapters and chapters of the mandatory portions of the *Jaiminīya*, which did not produce such sparks, are treated, just as Whitney and Oertel claimed, in a relatively uninspired fashion. Then, suddenly, something bursts out of the text in the form of a story. What impels it is a formalized fear.

Many of the stories in the *Jaiminīya* express fears that underlie dreams, myths, and rituals (such as the sacrifice). On the most basic level, these fears arise from human experience: people are afraid of the things that happen to them or that might happen to them. They may dream of these forces or events, and in their dreams they may express and exaggerate fears that are suppressed in waking life. These fears, either in their waking form or as they are transformed in dreams, may then undergo a further transformation into myths or rituals or both. The relationship between private dreams and public myths is a complex one, which I have discussed elsewhere (O'Flaherty 1984). What is relevant here is that dreams are expressed in one way in myths and in another way in rituals. Myths are closer to dreams than rituals are, both in their narrative structure and in their ability to express the fantastic, and the power of their symbolism is therefore more intense. Myths express untamed dangers; they give vent to the full range of nightmare possibilities. Rituals tend to tame those dangers and to express them in terms of a more limited range of human actions. The fears that appear in the waking experiences or the dreams of individuals are channeled into the sacrifice in order to make them public and to make them safe. By ordering and structuring these fears (either as they arise directly from experience or as they appear in dreams, where they have already undergone a primary transformation), rituals allow people to order and structure their reactions to these dangers in real life; they allow them to create a framework that they can then reintroduce into real experience. Participating in the formalized structures of someone else's funeral provides us with a framework within which to contemplate our own death. Or, to use J. Z. Smith's example, the memory of a bear-hunting ritual gives the hunters a sense of order that they carry with them the next time they hunt a bear (J. Z. Smith 1982, pp. 53–65).

But the ritual itself introduces new dangers and new fears. What happens if the ritual itself does not work, if the bears rush in and break up the bear-hunting ritual? This can happen, after all. It happens in a parable by Kafka (related to me by A. K. Ramanujan as a metaphor for cultural assimilation): Certain people performing a ceremony found that leopards kept interrupting it by breaking into the sacrificial area to drink the sacred water; when this happened often enough, the leopards were made part of the ceremony. In Vedic India, the demons that threaten the sacrifice have indeed become part of the ceremony; a significant proportion of the energy of the Brāhmaṇa priests is devoted to fending off the demons and to repairing the breaks that they make in the sacrifice, and this activity is part of the ritual. Nor does the only danger come from the fact that one may fail to carry out the ritual properly. The power aroused by the correctly performed ritual may get out of hand: the forces created to control bears may be harder to control than the bears. For, as the stories make unmistakably clear, the ritual itself involves potentially fatal dangers, and these must be added to the dangers that would threaten the sacrificer in normal life. These double dangers are always ready to pounce on the sacrificer and ruin his ritual and his life. Sometimes these dangers are personified as the demons (Rakṣases or Rākṣasas) who break into the sealed sacrifice and pollute it from outside; but they may also come from within, from the sacrificer himself, from the pollution inherent in his human vulnerability and mortality. And, finally, there are always nagging doubts that even the perfect ritual cannot really succeed in conquering death and danger (see B. K. Smith, 1984).

The Vedic sacrifice was designed primarily to allay the fear of death; through the sacrifice, a man could become immortal: "Deliver me from death, not from immortality" (*RV* 7. 59. 12; cf. *ŚPB* 2. 6. 1. 12; *AV* 18. 3). But death still held all of its sting in the *Ṛg Veda*; one hoped only to escape premature death, to live out a full life-span (usually conceived of as seventy or a hundred years), never to live forever. The Brāhmaṇas, by contrast, attempted to tame death by gradual degrees, first to enable the sacrificer to live out a full life-span, then to allow him to live for a hundred years or a thousand years, and finally to attain some sort of vaguely conceived complete immortality: "Whoever knows this conquers recurring death and attains a life-span; this is freedom from death in the other world and life here" (*ŚPB* 10. 2. 6. 190). But one can never be made entirely safe from death; there is always the danger that one will not succeed in completing the sacrifice that will grant immortality, that one will die before the end of the sacrifice:

> When Prajāpati was creating living beings, evil Death overpowered him. He performed asceticism for a thousand years, striving to leave that evil behind him, and in the thousandth year he purified himself entirely; the evil that he washed clean is his body. But what man could obtain a life of a thousand years? The man who knows this truth can obtain a thousand years. [*ŚPB* 10. 4. 4. 1–3; cf. O'Flaherty 1976, p. 217]

In a typical pattern of the Brāhmaṇas, this text first states the danger (that the ritual to procure immortality may be interrupted by death) and then breaks the vicious circle: "whoever knows this" (a phrase we will often encounter in the *Jaiminīya*) will live long enough to accomplish the dangerous ritual. Thus the Brāhmaṇas attempted to reassure the sacrificer that he had no reason to fear death.

But the persistence of these fears leads to the construction of myths about rituals, myths that attempt to tame the ritual that attempts to tame the fears. These myths are, by and large, what we have in the Brāhmaṇas. Some of them are meta-myths, thrice removed from the raw fears that fueled them: they are myths about rituals about dreams. Some are even further removed: they are myths about rituals about myths about dreams. Some are more direct: they are myths about the same experiences that provided the source of the ritual. The *Jaiminīya* stories are myths about the Vedic sacrifice, but they may also incorporate meanings from all the other parts of the continuum: direct experience, dreams, and myths.

The dangers that are sensed in dreams are reflected in the sacrifice; the brutality of dreams is reflected in the brutality of the sacrifice. The sacrifice, for example, reawakens our awareness of the sufferings of animals, but then it produces a ritual designed to dull that awareness, to smother it with ritual detail and thus to deflect it. The *Jaiminīya* stories of animal sacrifice (such as "Bhṛgu's Journey in the Other World" [*JB* 1. 42–44]) comment on the way in which the sacrifice attempts to assuage that potential guilt. Death and sex cannot, ultimately, be made safe; but they can at least be made formal, and that is what the ritual does. The myth about the ritual then stirs up a few ripples on the smooth surface of that formality, expressing not only the smoldering fears that the ritual cannot entirely extinguish but the additional fear inspired by the dangers implicit in the ritual itself—the fear that it will fail.

In this sense, the stories that the *Jaiminīya* introduces into the ritual undo something of what is done by the ritual itself: they unravel the ritual the way Penelope unravels her own weaving every night. To the extent that the ritual tends to conceal, by its mass of formal detail, the naked fear of death and danger, the stories that explicitly act out those fears are decoding the ritual even as the priests are encoding it. The stories introduce a kind of secondary elaboration, a commentary, into the dream itself, the ritual scenario.

It is ironical that Max Müller, though he sensed the dreamlike element in the Brāhmaṇas, regarded it as simply another instance of twaddle:

> Where the Brāhmaṇas or Āraṇyakas allude to grammatical, metrical, or etymological questions, they give nothing but theological and mystical dreams. So far from receiving elucidation, the points in question generally become involved in still greater darkness. [Müller 1860, p. 116]

Even in the twentieth century, Indologists have tended both to note and to sneer at the element of dreams in the Brāhmaṇas:

> One's first reading of a Brāhmaṇa is an extraordinary experience. It seems as if the men who composed these interminable gossiping lectures had left realities far behind them, and were living in a dreary realm of shadowy gods and men and topsy-turvy morality and religion, in which nothing belongs to the world we know except the sacrificial meats and drinks and the fees paid to the priestly dreamers. Yet in the midst of this waste of arid ritualism and childish speculation one finds the beginnings of grammar, of astronomy, of etymology, and of the philosophy of the *ātman*. There are also legends and narratives which are forerunners of the Epic, and numerous rules of conduct out of which finally arose the Hindu *dharma*. The Indian mind was by no means dead, although sacerdotalism was drunk with supremacy and in its folly and arrogance was hastening the day of revolt. [Farquhar 1920, p. 27]

Though Farquhar rejects the dreary realm of unreality depicted in the Brāhmaṇas, he does at least value their legends and narratives—their realistic legends and narratives, one assumes (forerunners of the martial Epic), rather than the surreal episodes that are characteristic of the *Jaiminīya*. And, above all, he is interested, like Max Müller fifty years before him, in grammar and etymology—in the genders of words, not those of demons.

But now our tastes have changed. Since Freud, many of us find the mystical and priestly dreams not only not arid or childish but full of a vivid reality of a different kind. For it was Freud who first pointed out the importance of stories about fathers and sons, about brothers, about mothers; the importance of symbols of animals; the importance of metaphors of breasts and penises; the importance of dreams. I selected the stories that I selected, and grouped them as I grouped them, because of certain ideas about patterns of human emotion that I learned from reading Freud. But aside from that initial bias, I found that a more detailed Freudian analysis contributed little, for the stories seemed self-explanatory and mutually illuminating. This is in part because they raise to the manifest level much of what is latent in Western literature. But it is also because they are about matters that Freud himself demonstrated to be basic to the human condition and therefore accessible to understanding across cultural barriers: they are about conflicts within the nuclear family, fears of danger from sexual contact, and the primacy of images of the body.

This book is about the problems, fears, and dangers (real and imaginary) that are reflected in our dreams and in the ancient Indian sacrifice. It is about the ways in which fear is transfigured first by dreams, then by rituals, then by folk narratives, and finally by learned storytellers. It is about the formalization of nightmares.

The Individuality of the *Jaiminīya Brāhmaṇa*

The question then arises, Whose nightmares and dreams are these? Are they personal nightmares or cultural nightmares? Is the psychology of the *Jaiminīya* a portrait of the artist as priest or the psychological profile of ancient Indian folklore? The artist uses folklore in a "nonfolk" way; for one thing, he tells the stories in Sanskrit, which is the farthest cry from a vernacular (though some form of Sanskrit was a spoken language at various times). But even the "folk"—the original tellers of the tale—had some sort of art; the story does not exist in nature, like a charming piece of driftwood, even if the events do (and of course no events exist *culturally* unless a teller of tales sees them happen). A folktale is not a dream, though an artist may turn a private dream into a culturally shared myth. So too, when we say that the *Jaiminīya* was composed by a "school" of the *Sāma Veda*, we cannot mean that the stories were put together by a committee (as the camel is sometimes said to have been), like a blackmail note composed by a group of conspirators, each supplying a letter in each word. Although the *Jaiminīya* as a whole may well have been composed, or at least redacted, by more than one priestly author, much like the King James Bible, this cannot have been the way in which the individual stories in it were composed. Somebody, somewhere, chose those words to tell it in, even if others took it up or added to it.

The arbitrary, albeit already highly charged, structure of the ritual provided a kind of springboard from which a specific personality could break out of the constraints of a very traditional art. The stories are the place where we can catch the priests with their masks down, the point at which we begin to see a personality behind the text. To study the imagery of the *Jaiminīya* stories and to set it against the more conventional imagery of the other Brāhmaṇas is to search for the moment when the storyteller's own obsessions break through, when his personal spirit transcends the frozen formulae, even as we can see how Homer transcends his inherited formulae and uses them, almost against themselves, to tell the old story in his own way. So, too, when we hear a great jazz improviser play "Muskat Ramble" or "Royal Garden Blues," we appreciate his individual genius *because* we have heard these same pieces done hundreds of times by less-gifted musicians; and because we know the conventions of the music by heart, we can see what is not conventional in his rendition. The conventions, by their very strictness, thus provide a kind of freedom. Of all the musical improvisations that I know, the most elaborate expression is found in the Indian *rāga*, with its infinite variations upon a single theme.

Yet ultimately it is useless to try to separate the psychology of the artist from the psychology of the folk (though it is not, perhaps, useless to try to separate the art of the artist from the art of the folk). The same argument that is used, rightly, to justify the practice of regarding a "borrowed" folktale as part of the culture and psychology of the civilization that borrows it can surely be used to justify the practice of regarding a reworked folktale as indicative of the psychology of the artist who borrows it: if he takes it up and uses it, it has meaning for *him*. But this technique does not work so well in the other direction: one cannot so easily assume that the story means for the culture at large what it means for the artist. For one thing, it may be possible to demonstrate a kind of obsession in the artist on the grounds of statistical concentration: of all the things that the culture offers him, why does he select these particular things over and over? It is possible, of course, to do something along similar lines for the culture at large; thus Sudhir Kakar has demonstrated that India has a particular taste for certain types of stories that occur, though rarely, in clinical practice elsewhere (Kakar 1978); one might well regard these as cultural obsessions. But without a knowledge of *all* the stories told in a particular time and place in India (a hypothetical situation that is not even ideally possible, let alone practical), it would be hard to sort out the clusters; nor is it by any means self-evident that quantitative dominance is a sufficient ground on which to establish psychological dominance. What about repression, for instance? What about the stories the artist *avoids*? It is, I think, madness to try to draw precise conclusions about the personality of an ancient author, let alone an ancient school, merely by analyzing his formal texts; but it is possible to determine what he was particularly interested in.

To understand the folklore and the character of the *Jaimi-*

nīya is to understand the delicate balance between, and intersection of, the general (folklore: themes that occur widely not only in India but also in other cultures) and the particular (individuality: the thoughts of this particular author or school). These two, of course, overlap; for one can understand "the general psychology of the folk" of India in terms of the recurrent concerns expressed by stories told all over the world, just as one can understand it in terms of the recurrent concerns expressed by one particular Indian author or group of authors.

The stories in the *Jaiminīya* that can be traced back to the *Ṛg Veda* are there merely sketched, powerfully but briefly. We can surmise that, in the time of the *Ṛg Veda*, these stories were told in detail in popular versions, but we have no trace of these and can only speculate about their nature. They must have been very different from the stories in the *Jaiminīya*, which is the first fully expressed version of them that we have. For the old gory, chaotic, heroic world of Vedic sacrifice (as Jan Heesterman described it to me) bred these stories in its violent, passionate way; but then they had somehow to be artificially flattened in order to bring them into the two-dimensional, ordered, never-never world of the sacrifice in the Brāhmaṇas. One could argue, as A. K. Ramanujan has argued with me, that Eggeling and Whitney were *right*: that the flattening process ruins the stories; that the stories as they appear in the *Jaiminīya* have lost their point. It is true that the *Jaiminīya* stories are generally of the shaggy-dog variety: after endless dangers and troubles, it suddenly turns out that there was really no problem after all. The reader may recall the character portrayed by Melina Mercouri in the film *Never on Sunday*: she retold all the old Greek tragedies and gave each one a happy ending, usually one in which everyone (Jason and Medea and the children, for example) went off for a day at the seashore. The *Jaiminīya* tends to turn the Vedic tragedies into stories with happy endings; this is particularly apparent in the usual punch line, which is a purely formulaic expression: "He saw this chant and praised with it and found success."

By gearing all of his stories to the sacrifice, the author of the *Jaiminīya* is committed to the happy ending of whatever story he chooses to tell. The story may be one that has a happy ending in the folk source from which the *Jaiminīya* takes it, or it may be one that is meant to end in tragedy. In either case, the *Jaiminīya* author has no choice about his ending, and so he cannot choose to depict a complete tragedy. There is incidental tragedy, and incidental suffering, in the *Jaiminīya*—everywhere but at the end. The climax does occur, but it does not occur at the spot where the Western reader, or even the Western folklorist, is accustomed to look for it. The closest parallel that one might find in the West would be in the last comedies of Shakespeare, where the dark events unfold with seemingly unrelenting intimations of doom until the last moment, when all is made, sometimes rather unconvincingly, right (Grene 1969a). Tragedy uses an aesthetic form to create the image of meaning in pain. The *Jaiminīya* cannot do this. Instead, it creates the image of order and the liquidation of pain. Yet, in either case, the pain—and the fear, and the danger—is vividly portrayed.

What characterizes even the Greek tragedies, however, is not their endings (which are occasionally, though not usually, happy) but the view of human life within which the story takes place. The Brāhmaṇas have a tragic view of life; this is intrinsic in the images of violence that provide the background for the sacrifice. But the Brāhmaṇas suggest a practical way of dealing with a life that is constantly threatened by danger. When they take the sacrificial chaos of the Vedas and make it all neat and tidy (which is what the Brāhmaṇas *do* to sacrifice), they may make it into a "controlled catastrophe" (again in Jan Heesterman's phrase), but it is still a catastrophe. And I do not think that this transformation necessarily spoils the story. The *Jaiminīya* is muted; the excitement is there, but it is stated in curiously flat tones. If the vibrant palette of the Vedas could be likened to that of German expressionism, the tone of the Brāhmaṇas could be likened to the technique of Dali or Magritte: always controlled, careful in its detail, it reveals a world all the more passionate and surreal because it is suppressed. The stories in the Brāhmaṇas have become mnemotechnic devices to order the jungle growth of chants, but they have the power to trigger, with formal detail, the full emotional range that is built into the ritual. This is, I think, true of the Brāhmaṇas' understatement in general, but it is particularly true of the *Jaiminīya*, where the stories often break out of the rigid sacerdotal mold and sprout new images of great emotional power before lapsing back into the cooler tone of the genre. Ramanujan has suggested that the stories that the *Jaiminīya* flattens (in comparison with their putative Vedic originals) are then made tumescent again in the *Mahābhārata*, as the dried Soma plant was reinfused with water and milk before it was pressed for the Vedic sacrifice. I think the *Jaiminīya* stories are better than that. They may be flattened, but they are not dried; they are merely concentrated. The *Mahābhārata* often brings out the implications that are already present in the *Jaiminīya* stories *in nuce*, much as one adds hot water to a concentrated cube of chicken soup. I happen to prefer the *Jaiminīya* versions, hard and compressed, to the watered-down Epic. But the reader may judge for himself, after reading the *Jaiminīya* and *Mahābhārata* versions side by side (for example, the stories of "Trita and His Brothers" [*JB* 1. 184], "The Rejuvenation of Cyavana" [*JB* 3. 120–29], and "The Brahmin's Wife with Hair on the Soles of Her Feet" [*JB* 2. 269–72]).

Method of Proceeding

After telling each story, one can place it in a context by shining a light on it from several different directions (or, to mix the metaphor, by tying it down with several different ropes).

1. *Backwards*. One can seek the roots of the Brāhmaṇas in the *Ṛg Veda* (and other Vedas). I have done this as little as possible, drawing on the *Ṛg Veda* only when the Brāhmaṇa itself does so explicitly or when a point that makes little sense in the Brāhmaṇa is clarified by reference to the *Ṛg Veda*. In

"The Charioteer and the Vanishing Fire" (*JB* 3. 94–96), for example, the plot as adumbrated in the *Ṛg Veda* lends power and cogency to the *Jaiminīya* retelling. But in general one can assume that the author of the *Jaiminīya* knew the *Ṛg Veda* (or at least the *Sāma Veda*, which contains much of the *Ṛg Veda*) very well indeed, probably by heart, and that, as with the general corpus of ancient Indian folklore, he simply selected the parts that suited his purposes. Knowing what he selected from does not, therefore, increase our knowledge of his general intent, except when he takes pains to sidestep an obviously relevant Ṛg Vedic component of his story.

2. *Forwards*. One can trace the later history of the story in the Hindu Epics and Purāṇas. Here too, due to the unbroken thread of tradition from guru to pupil (the *parampara*), it is quite likely that certain obscurities in the *Jaiminīya* are in fact correctly resolved in later texts; but, again, I have resorted to those texts only when the *Jaiminīya* was not fully comprehensible in itself. I have, however, given three *Mahābhārata* stories to compare with the *Jaiminīya* versions of the tales of Trita, Cyavana, and the Brahmin's wife, as noted above. Moreover, I have supplied an appendix (Appendix 1), indicating which stories from the *Jaiminīya* appear in other Vedic texts or in the *Mahābhārata*, in order to support my contention that the *Jaiminīya* is the missing link between many stories told first in the *Ṛg Veda* and later in the *Mahābhārata*.

3. *Sideways*. One can compare the *Jaiminīya* with other Brāhmaṇas. This is essential to one's understanding of the *Jaiminīya* folklore (for it establishes the place of the *Jaiminīya* in the context of a group of texts roughly contemporaneous with it) and of its individuality (for it shows how this particular author or group of authors wanted to put something into the story when no one else at that time chose to put it in). I have drawn on all the relevant variants of each story in other Brāhmaṇas and have cited them where they seem illuminating. On some occasions the argument from silence is even more useful: no one but the *Jaiminīya* author tells the story at

all. This, like Sherlock Holmes's negative formulation ("Why *didn't* the dog bark?"), is never logically sound (there are so many possible reasons for a dog *not* to bark), but it is nevertheless suggestive. The noisier argument (why the dog *did* bark, or why other Brāhmaṇas do tell the story but in another way) is far more substantial, though it may not necessarily be more significant.

4. *Up*. One can look at other folktales throughout the world, dealing with the same theme. I have not followed this line in my analysis of the stories, but an awareness of world folklore was very much at the heart of the selection process: I chose stories that were not merely Indian stories. To give a general indication of the range of such distribution, I have supplied an appendix (Appendix 3) in which I link some of the central *Jaiminīya* stories to Stith Thompson's index of motifs and his index of tale types. This appendix might also allow the reader to follow up a cross-cultural comparative study, which would extend the basis of my present inquiry—Why is the *Jaiminīya* different from all other Brāhmaṇas?—to a more challenging, but unwieldy, inquiry: Why is Indian folklore different from all other folklores? (a subject that A. K. Ramanujan has already broached [Ramanujan 1981]).

5. *Down*. One can probe for the deep meaning of the story, in India or in the human heart. This is the ultimate goal of any study of religion or literature, and it is my goal here. To pursue the analysis on this level, I have used other lights (or ropes) accessible to me: world literature, Indian culture, Vedic mythology, psychology; and I encourage the reader to call on his or her own similar resources.

Although I have often found it useful to begin with the procedure sanctioned by traditional Indian philology in glossing each text—backwards to the *Ṛg Veda* and sideways to the other Brāhmaṇas—I have organized the book along the lines of what I regard as the more important axes of the stories, the ups and downs. These are reflected in the themes of the basic fears and dangers that arise out of dreams and flow into the sacrifice: the fear of death and old age, the fear of mutilation by the angry father, and the fear of women.

A final note on technical matters. In giving each story, I have translated quite literally but not completely. That is, I have omitted certain passages in the longer stories—principally, but not only, passages dealing with details of the sacrifice and passages containing verbatim repetitions, such as direct discourse (where someone repeats a conversation, I may simply say, "She told him what they had said"). But the passages that I have translated, I have translated pretty much word for word, except that I have substituted ordinary words for certain highly technical terms (I have used "priest," for example, to translate Udgātṛ, Adhvaryu, etc.). Aside from these indulgences, the translations are strict, being far closer to those that I produced for the Penguin sourcebooks (*Hindu Myths, The Rig Veda*) than to those that I used in books (about Śiva, Evil, Dreams, and Women) where I was adducing many myths in order to demonstrate certain arguments.

In other words, I regard this present book as a kind of sourcebook for Brāhmaṇa folklore, not as a book demonstrating a theory about Brāhmaṇa folklore. The theory, *tout court*, is that the *Jaiminīya* is a sourcebook of ancient Indian folklore and that the folktales it contains are the oldest of those recorded in India and are thus among the oldest in the world. More particularly, my hypothesis is that the author(s) of the *Jaiminīya* had a unique ability to draw on folklore in order to dramatize, in the context of the sacrificial ritual, the same nightmare fears that the sacrifice was designed to conceal and to control. The *Jaiminīya* uses folktales to draw out of the ritual the dark human feelings that are hidden deep within it, just as one might use a flame to draw from a piece of parchment a message encoded on it in invisible ink.

2
The Fear of Death

The tale of Bhṛgu is the story of a boy's encounter with death and his realization of the power of the sacrifice to stave death off. Of all the stories in the *Jaiminīya*, it is perhaps the most famous, the most explicitly symbolic, and the most important to subsequent Indian religious literature. It is a story of fathers and sons, of the death and revival of a son, of the struggle with death, of the symbolism of dreams, and of the encounter with dangerous women. It is a wonderful story, though rather a long one.

Bhṛgu's Journey in the Other World (*JB* 1. 42–44)

Bhṛgu, the son of Varuṇa, was devoted to learning. He thought that he was better than his father, better than the gods, better than the other Brahmins who were devoted to learning. Varuṇa thought to himself, "My son does not know anything at all. Come, let us teach him to know something." He took away his life's breaths, and Bhṛgu fainted and went beyond this world.

Bhṛgu arrived in the world beyond. There he saw a man cut another man to pieces and eat him. He said, "Has this really happened? What is this?" They said to him, "Ask Varuṇa, your father. He will tell you about this." He came to

a second world, where a man was eating another man, who was screaming. He said, "Has this really happened? What is this?" They said to him, "Ask Varuṇa, your father. He will tell you about this." He went on to another world, where he saw a man eating another man, who was soundlessly screaming; then to another, where two women were guarding a great treasure; then to a fifth, where there were two streams flowing on an even level, one filled with blood and one filled with butter. A naked black man with a club guarded the stream filled with blood; out of the stream filled with butter, men made of gold were drawing up all desires with bowls of gold. In the sixth world there were five rivers with blue lotuses and white lotuses, flowing with honey like water. In them there were dancing and singing, the sound of the lute, crowds of celestial nymphs [Apsarases], a fragrant smell, and a great sound.

Bhṛgu returned from that world and came to Varuṇa, who said, "Did you arrive, my son?" "I arrived, father." "Did you see, my son?" "I saw, father." "What, my son?" "A man cut another man to pieces and ate him." "Yes," said Varuṇa; "when people in this world offer no oblation and lack true knowledge, but cut down trees and lay them on the fire, those trees take the form of men in the other world and eat [those people] in return." "How can one avoid that [*niṣkṛti*]?" "When you put fuel on the sacred fire, that is how you avoid it and are free of it.

"What [did you see] second?" "A man was eating another man, who was screaming." "Yes," he said; "when people in this world offer no oblation and lack true knowledge, but cook for themselves animals that cry out, those animals take the form of men in the other world and eat in return." "How can one avoid that?" "When you offer the first oblation with the voice, that is how you avoid it and are free of it.

"What third?" "A man ate another man, who was soundlessly screaming." "Yes," he said; "when people in this world offer no oblation and lack true knowledge, but cook for themselves rice and barley, which scream soundlessly, that rice and barley take the form of men in the other world and eat in return." "How can one avoid that?" "When you offer the last oblation with the mind, that is how you avoid it and are free of it.

"What fourth?" "Two women were guarding a great treasure." "Yes," said he, "they were Faith and Nonfaith. When people in this world offer no oblation and lack true knowledge, but sacrifice without faith, that [sacrifice] goes to Nonfaith; what [they sacrifice] with faith goes to Faith." "How can one avoid that?" "When you eat with your thumb, you avoid it and are free of it.

"What fifth?" "Two streams were flowing on an even level, one filled with blood and one filled with butter. A naked black man with a club guarded the stream filled with blood; men made of gold were drawing up all desires with bowls of gold out of the stream filled with butter." "Yes," said he; "when people in this world offer no oblation and lack true knowledge, but squeeze out the blood of a Brahmin, that is the river of blood; and the naked black man who guarded it with a club is Anger, whose food is that [blood]." "How can one avoid that?" "When you eat with a sacrificial spoon, you avoid it and are free of it. And when you wash out the spoon and pour the water out toward the north, that is the river of butter; and out of that [butter] the men made of gold draw up all desires with bowls of gold.

"What sixth?" "Five rivers, with blue lotuses and white lotuses, flowed with honey like water; in them there were dancing and singing, the sound of the lute, crowds of celestial nymphs, a fragrant smell, and a great sound." "Yes," said he; "those were my own worlds." "How can one get that?" "By dipping in five times and drawing out five times." Then he added, "There is no chance of getting worlds except by the oblation [*agnihotra*]. Today I am fasting before building the sacrificial fire." And they made it for him in that way. Whoever offers the oblation with this true knowledge, he is not eaten in return by trees who take the form of men in the

other world, nor by animals, nor by rice and barley; nor do his good deeds and sacrifices go to Faith and Nonfaith. He wards off the streams of blood and wins the streams of butter.

Before going on to analyze this story in the context of its prehistory in the *Ṛg Veda* (the view backwards), and its post-history in the *Mahābhārata* (the view forwards), let us look sideways at the only extant parallel text, that of the *Śatapatha Brāhmaṇa* (11. 6. 1. 1–13). Since it is long, though not as long as the *Jaiminīya*, I will simply point out a few salient differences in the *Śatapatha* version:

1. Varuṇa does not kill Bhṛgu or send him to other worlds; he sends him simply to the five directions (East, South, West, North, and upward) to see what he can see.
2. The people in each world give Bhṛgu the explanations of the meaning of their actions; he does not have to wait to get home and ask his father, as he does in the *Jaiminīya*.
3. After the fourth direction, there is just one final scene in the world reached "upward": two women, one beautiful and one ugly, stand on either side of a black man with yellow eyes, who holds a club. When Bhṛgu sees this, he goes home in terror.

In all three of these variations, the *Śatapatha* is less dramatic than the *Jaiminīya*. In particular, the *Śatapatha* entirely omits the final scene, the one positive scene: the heaven in contrast with all the previous hells; it simply sends Bhṛgu "up" to the final world, which combines the fourth and fifth scenes of the *Jaiminīya*. The symbolism of the sixth scene in the *Jaiminīya*—the scene omitted from *Śatapatha*—is quite clear, though it is never glossed in the text; it is the world of complete sensual and sexual satiation—the father's world as viewed by the son. And the way it is won—by "dipping in and pulling out"—has a patent sexual meaning in addition to its manifest sacrificial meaning (dipping in and out with the sacrificial spoon that is the subject of the previous explanation). By adding this heaven to the hells, and by stating that it is the *father's* heaven, the *Jaiminīya* uses the context to highlight the human dimension—the son's view of the father's life—that is the implicit counterpart of the divine dimension; for the world of Bhṛgu's father is the world of the god Varuṇa.

The central scenes in both texts deal with eating. Dangers arise in the context of incorrect profane eating and are warded off by correct sacred eating. Indeed, the two are inextricably linked by the ancient Indian belief that it is wrong to take food without offering some, at least mentally, to the gods; in the broadest sense, all human food consists of divine leftovers. The meaning of food in the story of Bhṛgu can best be understood through a step-by-step analysis of each scene.

In the first scene, men dismember other men and eat them. These men are the trees; and by laying firewood on the sacrificial fire, one avoids this fate, The fact that the trees eat the men in the other world, whereas in this world men do not eat trees, makes sense if one defines the transformed objects not as literal food but as the things that men use in preparing food (fuel, water for cooking, and so forth), or, in a still broader sense, as the numinous objects that are the sources of fertility. Trees, cattle, plants, water and women are the substances with which the primary transactions and transferrals of positive and negative power take place in ancient India (O'Flaherty 1976, pp. 153–60); these five substances are therefore ideally suited for transferring the roles of active eaters and passive "eatens" from one to the other.

In the second world, the men who are cut up are screaming; they are animals or cattle, who bellow (though not at the moment of sacrifice, for then they are suffocated). The people who are eaten in silence in the third world are sacrificial rice and barley; the way to avoid this world is to offer a second oblation, mentally, for the silent meditation is analogous to the helpless silence in which vegetables are eaten. One is reminded of the writings of the great Indian botanist, Jagadis Chandra Bose, who "demonstrated, at the Royal Institution in 1901, the death agony of a poisoned tinfoil" (Nandy 1980, p. 47), and who moved George Bernand Shaw deeply with his demonstration of an "unfortunate carrot strapped to the table of an unlicensed vivisector" (ibid., p. 63). The screaming and the silence in the Sanskrit text have the quality of a true nightmare, the nightmare from which Bhṛgu flees.

The three final worlds of the *Jaiminīya* are given rather abstract glosses in comparison with the vivid symbolism of the rest of the text: the women are Faith and Nonfaith, and the man is Anger. Each of the three final worlds has positive elements, the first two in a dialectic contrast with negative elements, so that they form a kind of transition from all the negative hells to the entirely positive final world. That world is a heaven, opposed to the unequivocal hells of the first three worlds. Thus Faith, the river of butter, and the rivers of honey in which the nymphs gambol are all part of the worlds that one hopes to win, while Nonfaith, the river of blood, and all the early worlds are the ones that one hopes to avoid.

A. Weber suggested that the women, Faith and Nonfaith, may originally have represented the dispensers of good and evil (Weber 1855, p. 29). This contention is supported by a story in the *Mahābhārata* that bears a strong resemblance to the tale of Bhṛgu:

> **When Uttanka's teacher's wife tried to seduce him, and Uttanka resisted her, the teacher was pleased; but the wife sent him on a dangerous errand that brought him to the underworld. There he saw two women who were weaving a cloth with black and white threads, and a wheel being turned by six boys, and a handsome man who told him to blow into the anus of a horse. When Uttanka returned home and asked his teacher, "What does this mean?" the teacher replied, "Those two women were the One-that-Places and the One-that-Disposes; the black and white threads are night and day, the wheel is the year, and the six boys are the six seasons. And the man is the rain god, and the horse is the fire god."** [*MBh* **1. 3. 146–75]**

Though the scenes in the other world depict neither pleasure nor pain, the episode of the horse's ass is vividly physiological. In any case, the generally abstract tone of the *Mahābhārata* passage (shattered only by that one earthy incident) leads the author to gloss the women in a highly abstract way. But when one takes into account the way in which the *Jaiminīya* analogizes the two women to butter and blood, it becomes possible to connect them with the good and evil forms of the mother and the whore, the mother who gives milk (butter) and the whore who drinks blood (semen) (O'Flaherty 1980a, pp. 21–22, 40–43). If these deep meanings are read into a text in which everything must have a sacrificial counterpart, Faith and Nonfaith are bland but workable labels for what is desired and what is feared.

The *Jaiminīya* says that one avoids the world of these women by eating with the thumb. This is quite appropriate. Since one is dealing with women in the context of food and with the parallels between food and sex, the thumb may be symbolic of the nourishing breast (as it is in the tale "The Uncle Who Tried to Murder the Newborn Child" [*JB* 3. 221]). Thus one conquers these women and avoids their world by eating them—symbolically and sacrificially.

It is worth noting, as Sudhir Kakar has suggested, two emphases in the depiction of Bhṛgu's heavens and hells. First, as is typical of Indian cosmologies, the hells are depicted far more vividly than the heavens: the hells come first, there are more of them, and they are described in greater detail than the heavens. Second, the emphasis even in the heavens is on the pleasure of food rather than the pleasures of sex. Indeed, as Kakar remarks, "In any case, given the importance of food transgressions and 'oral guilt,' the nymphs will probably be eaten rather than ravished" (Sudhir Kakar, personal communication).

That the black man with yellow eyes symbolizes Anger is simple enough, but the rituals that protect one against him are more complex. The official rite to keep him away (drinking water or milk out of the spoon or ladle) works in a manner parallel to that which underlies the protection against the two women. But the water in the spoon takes on extra power from the implicit contrast with other liquids: the river of butter (which is the water tossed upwards) and the river of blood (which is the blood pressed out of Brahmins). The black man is probably a form of Yama, the god of the dead (who is often described as a black man with a golden club, and who is encountered by the hero in other Indian versions of the story of the journey to the other world). Blood would then naturally be his food. Gold, which here contrasts with the black of anger or the red of blood, is symbolic of immortality throughout the Brāhmaṇas. The golden men are not explicitly glossed here, but the context seems to indicate that they represent those who reap the benefits of good deeds in the other world.

What is the meaning of the *Jaiminīya* tale of Bhṛgu, as a whole? The basic point seems to be that the other world is the inverse of this world, a looking-glass world, upside down, reversing the roles of subject and object. This is, as Lommel has pointed out, a widespread folk motif, often applied to the world of death; it is also characteristic of the world of dreams. Lommel argues that there is no moralizing in this depiction, that the texts are not saying, "Do not eat animals, for then they will eat you," but, rather, "Be sure to eat animals in the right way, or they will eat you." There are no "expiations" or "atonements" at the end, for the Sanskrit term *niṣkṛti* describes not a remorseful attempt to suffer in order to pay for a sin but rather a careful plan by which to avoid making a mistake that will bring unwanted consequences. Being eaten in the other world, then, is not a punishment for sins but rather a straight reversal of the inevitable (and not condemned) eating in this world; just as right becomes left and up becomes down in the world of the dead, so the eater is eaten.

The retribution by which animals turn on those who have eaten them is an instance of the *lex talionis* (Oertel 1893, pp. 234–38; Oertel 1905a, p. 196; Lommel 1950, pp. 93–109; Oertel 1908, pp. 119–21). Thus the *Kauśītaki Brāhmaṇa* (*KB* 11. 3) states: "Just as in this world men eat cattle and devour them, so in the other world cattle eat men and devour them." So, too, it is said, "Whatever food a man eats in this world, that [food] eats him in the other world" (*ŚPB* 12. 9. 1. 1). This consequence may be avoided if one performs the appropriate sacrifice (*ŚKhB* 11. 3; *JB* 1. 26). The law books of Manu (5. 55) and the *Mahābhārata* (*MBh* 13. 117. 34) offer a pun on this subject: Flesh is called *māṃsa* because he (*sa*) eats me (*mām*) in the other world if I eat him now. A similar pun appears in the *Śukasaptati* (65, cited by Oertel 1908, p. 120), ingeniously translated by Charles Lanman: "*Me eat* in t'other world will he, whose *meat* in this world eat do I."

Another passage in the *Jaiminīya* describes a similar instance of reciprocity between men and animals, again without moralizing. This story appears in a passage explaining why the sacrificer should wear a red cowhide, a practice that is mentioned in other texts (*PB* 16. 1. 1–10; *KB* 25. 15).

How Men Changed Skins With Animals (*JB* 2. 182–83)

In the beginning, the skin of cattle was the skin of a man, and the skin of a man was the skin of cattle [i.e., cattle then had the skin that men now have, and the reverse]. Cattle could not bear the heat, rain, flies, and mosquitoes. They went to man and said, "Man, let this skin [of ours] be yours, and that skin [of yours] be ours." "What would be the result of that?" [man asked]. "We could be eaten by you," [the animals said], "and this [skin of ours] would be your clothing." So saying they gave [man] his clothing. Therefore, when [the sacrificer] puts on a red hide, he flourishes in that form. Then cattle do not eat him in the other world [if he wears the skin, they think he is one of them]; for cattle do eat a man in the other world [otherwise]. Therefore, one should not stand naked near a cow, for it is liable to run away from one, thinking, "I am bearing his skin [and he may try to get it back from me]." And this skin has got a tail, which makes it complete.

The transaction in the other world is here interpreted as the reversal of a reversal: men and cattle traded places long ago, and, as a result, cattle *willingly* undertook to supply men with food and clothing but also, apparently, won the boon of eating men (and, perhaps, flaying them) in the other world. To avoid this, the sacrificer pretends to restore things to the way they were *in illo tempore*: by stealing the cow's skin, he prevents her from stealing his; and by keeping her from seeing his own skin, he prevents her from fearing that he will steal hers (an act that, in fact, he constantly performs and one that it is the express purpose of this text to justify). The naked man beside the cow is reminiscent of the naked (black) man beside the river of butter in the tale of Bhṛgu. In retrospect, nakedness may bear in that tale some of the meanings it bears here: by reducing man to the level of the beasts, it makes him vulnerable to their sufferings when he enters the other world.

It is easy enough to see how this idea of reversals in the other world could, in fact, quickly become ethicized, how one could come to believe that the best way to avoid being eaten in the other world was not merely to eat animals in the proper (sacrificial) way but to stop eating them altogether. It is also apparent that the things that Bhṛgu sees in the other world could also be interpreted as a vision of the next life in *this* world. Thus one could (as Lommel does [1950, p. 97]) interpret the tale of Bhṛgu as a very early foreshadowing of the doctrine of reincarnation, which first appears explicitly in the Upaniṣads. As Gananath Obeyesekere has pointed out, if one adds the ethical hypothesis to the hypothesis of rebirth, one comes up with the doctrine of karma (Obeyesekere 1980). Indeed, Bhṛgu's experience in the other world set the pattern for what was to become an important set piece in Purāṇic literature: the interlocutor of the Purāṇa is presented with a lurid picture of the tortures in various hells, to which, he is assured, he will be sent because of his karma. In fear and trembling, he asks the narrator if there is not, in fact, some way of avoiding going to such a hell; curiously enough, there is, and the rest of the text is devoted to an exposition of whatever particular doctrine or ritual is being advertised at the moment. That the belief that men become reincarnated as animals should lead to vegetarianism is hardly surprising, though it is not, perhaps, inevitable; the corollary belief in reincarnation as plants would, on that model, lead to complete fasting. It is, I think, wrong to view the story of Bhṛgu as a text that espouses either the doctrine of karma or the ideals of noninjury or vegetarianism, though it is probably useful to point out the ways in which it could easily contribute to the rise of such doctrines.

The hell that Bhṛgu visits is not yet an Upaniṣadic rebirth or a Purāṇic hell; it is a Vedic otherworld, perhaps above the earth, perhaps below it, perhaps (as the *Śatapatha* version suggests) even on the same level. It is a hell from which one can return during this life, just as the Vedic heaven was a place from which the sacrificer usually wished to return (B. Smith 1984). In glossing the symbolism of the Bhṛgu story, we noted that the naked black man might be Yama, lord of the world of the dead. This possibility is supported by a Ṛg Vedic hymn (*RV* 10. 135) that may have been one of the sources of the tale of Bhṛgu. It cannot be regarded as a very direct source, for the *Jaiminīya* does not regard *Ṛg Veda* 10. 135 as the text of which it is a gloss (in contrast with the way in which "Vasiṣṭha's Dying Son and the Half-Verse" [*JB* 2. 392], for example, is regarded explicitly as a gloss on *Ṛg Veda* 7. 32. 26); but it may well have been present in the mind of the author of the *Jaiminīya* story of Bhṛgu. *Ṛg Veda* 10. 135 is somewhat obscure, but the plot seems to contain the following elements: The father of a young boy has died, and the boy mentally follows the journey of his father to the realm of Yama, grieving and trying to get him to return. The voice of the father or Yama tells the boy that the chariot that the boy has built in his imagination to follow his father is already, unknown to the boy, bringing him after his father. This chariot is the funeral sacrifice or the oblation that "carries" the corpse to Yama and the fathers (O'Flaherty 1981, pp. 55–56).

This Vedic hymn agrees with our text in only the very broadest outlines, such as the boy's journey to the world of death and his enlightenment by his father. But this outline supplies the basis of the story of Naciketas, which occupies the entire *Kaṭha Upaniṣad*:

> **Vājaśravasa gave all that he possessed, and while the sacrificial cows were being led up, Faith entered into Naciketas, and he thought, "Joyless are the worlds a man goes to when he gives such cows, milkless and barren." As he kept asking his father, "Daddy, whom will you give *me* to?" his father finally replied, "I give you to Yama!" Naciketas went to Yama's house and stayed there for three days before Yama returned. Having failed to provide the hospitality due to a Brahmin, Yama offered Naciketas three boons. Naciketas asked that his father might greet him, on his return, in a good mood, appeased, and no longer furious; and he asked Yama to teach him about the Naciketas sacrificial fire that leads to heaven and about what happens to a man after death. When Naciketas had received this knowledge from Yama, he became free from death. [*KU* 1–6; cf. *TB* 3. 11. 8. 1–6]**

When Naciketas's father becomes infuriated at his son's persistent questions (like Father William: "I have answered three questions and that is enough"), he curses him to go to Hell; Naciketas takes the curse literally, like the mother in "The Sick Boy in the Ditch" (*JB* 1. 151). That the father truly intended to harm the boy is evident from Naciketas's pitiful plea to Yama: with all the world to choose, and even the secret of immortality, he first chooses to have his father stop being cross with him. Naciketas, fearing that his father will not win a good heaven if he gives such poor cows, offers himself as a human sacrifice; in effect, the father accepts the offer. The barren cows provide a negative female image that is the equivalent of the black woman in the *Jaiminīya*; the positive female image is Faith, who enters Naciketas at the beginning, whereas Bhṛgu finds her only at the end, in his father's gloss.

Indeed, in the tale of Naciketas the gloss is provided not by his father at all but by Death himself; this is the form in which the tale usually appears in other cultures as well. In this variant, since the father is wrong, the father's "worlds" are poor (or so Naciketas fears), and it is the son who wins the sacred knowledge, not the father.

This reversal—the son is better than the father—occurs in another passage of the *Jaiminīya* that is closely related to the tale of Bhṛgu.

The Son Who Was Better Than His Father (*JB* 2. 160–61)

Ṛjiśvan, the son of Vātavat, undertook a sacrifice, but he fainted dead away. Then they sat down with Vṛṣaśuṣma, the young son of Ṛjiśvan, who had smeared his eyes [with butter]; they said, "Since this man died, we will complete this sacrifice with his son." But the son fainted and went to the world beyond, and in that world he came to his father.

The father had a beautiful world, and the son said, "Daddy, whose world is this?" "Mine," he said. And there was another, even more beautiful. "Whose is this?" "Yours," he said. The son said, "Daddy, since you have given more than I have and have studied more than I have, then how is it that this world is yours and that one is mine?" The father said, "My little son, this world is for those who have succeeded in carrying out their vows. Of the two of us, you have carried out your vow better than I have. Therefore, this is my world, and that is your world. Go back; you will complete the sacrifice. And whatever you desire, that desire will be fulfilled. But keep your fingers crossed [*vakritās tv evāngulīḥ kurutād iti*]." The son [returned to the world and] completed the sacrifice.

This story reverses many of the premises of the tale of Bhṛgu. The son sees the beauty of his father's world, as in the Bhṛgu story, but then he sees that his own world is even more beautiful; the father explains the meaning of the worlds to him, as in the Bhṛgu story, but the meaning is that the son is superior to the father. So, too, the son faints (*tatāma*), as Bhṛgu does, but the father faints dead away (*avatatāma*). (The son, realizing this, smears butter on his eyes, which symbolizes his mourning; in *RV* 10. 18. 7, a widow smears butter on her eyes at her husband's funeral.) In "The Son Who Was Better Than His Father," the son merely outlives his father (as sons usually do); in other tales from the *Jaiminīya*, which we will encounter in chapter four, the son outthinks his father. Even in the *Ṛg Veda* there are several passages that suggest that the son may sometimes surpass his father (*RV* 1. 164. 16 and 18; 4. 9. 2; O'Flaherty 1981, pp. 77–78). But the tale of Bhṛgu defends the more traditional Vedic order, the heroic order, in which fathers are greater than their sons. In this corpus, the aggression usually begins with the father's attack upon the son, but the son survives the attack.

Other Brāhmaṇas also contain stories that help us understand the tale of Bhṛgu. In one of these—the following tale from the *Jaiminīya Upaniṣad Brāhmaṇa*—the role of the father is filled by an uncle; here, as in the Ṛg Vedic hymn of the boy and the chariot (RV 10. 135), and unlike the tale of Bhṛgu, it is the father rather than the son who dies and goes to the land of the dead. But, as in the Ṛg Vedic hymn as well as in the tale of Bhṛgu, it is also the older man who instructs the son.

THE GHOST OF THE BELOVED UNCLE (*JUB* 3. 6. 1–3)

Uccaiḥśravas Kaupayeya was a king of the Kurus; Keśin Dārbhya, king of the Pāñcālas, was his sister's son; they loved each other dearly. When Uccaiḥśravas Kaupayeya had departed from this world, Keśin Dārbhya went hunting in the woods, hoping to dispel his sadness. As he was roaming about, following the deer, he saw Uccaiḥśravas right between [him and the deer]. He said to him, "Have I gone crazy, or am I right?" "You haven't gone crazy," Uccaiḥśravas said. "You know. I am who you think I am." "Yes," said Keśin,

"they say, 'If someone [dead] appears [here], others go to his world.' But how were you able to appear to me?" "True," said Uccaiḥśravas; "when I found the guardian of that world, I became visible to you; for I thought, 'I will dispel his sadness, and I will teach him.'" "Yes," said he; "now let me embrace you." But as he tried to embrace him, he escaped him as if he were approaching smoke or wind or space or the gleam of fire. He could not get hold of him to embrace him.

Then Keśin said, "You have now the very same form that you used to have, but I cannot get hold of you to embrace you." "True," he said; "a Brahmin who knew the chant sang it for me, and by means of that disembodying chant he shook off my body. If someone who knows that chant sings it for you, he sends you to the same world that the gods live in." Keśin said, "Patanga Prājāpatya was a beloved son of Prajāpati. His father taught him that chant, and he sang it for the sages, and they shook off their bodies." "Yes," said the other; "and Prajāpati sang the same chant for the gods, and the gods above shook off their bodies." Uccaiḥśravas instructed Keśin about this chant, and then he said, "Have a man who knows this chant sing it for you."

Then Keśin went away and wandered about, questioning the Brahmins of the Kurus and the Pāñcālas. He said to them, "I am going to perform a twelve-day sacrifice with the meters transposed. If any of you knows the chant that I know, he shall sing it for me. Think about this." They thought about it, but not a single one of them could give him the answer he wanted. So he kept wandering about in this way, and then one day he came upon a man who was lying on his funeral litter in a burning-ground, engaged in a secret ritual. And this man's shadow had not left him. Keśin said to him, "Who are you?" "I am a Brahmin, Prātṛda Bhālla." "What knowledge do you have?" "The chant." "Good," said Keśin; "I am going to perform a twelve-day sacrifice with the meters transposed. If you know the chant that I know, you will sing it for me. Think about this." He thought about it and gave him the answer that he wanted.

Then Keśin said of him, "This is the man who will sing for me." But the Brahmins of the Kurus and Pāñcālas were jealous and resented the man; they said, "Is he going to sing for you, when these Brahmins of your own good family are here? For whom is he good enough?" "He's good enough for me," said Keśin. And the man sang the chant well enough; and so they call him the "Good-Enough Chanter."

Perhaps precisely because Uccaiḥśravas is *not* Keśin's father and hence has no reason to compete with him, as fathers and sons so often do in India, their relationship is purely a loving one (though a counterinstance is provided by the tale of "The Uncle Who Tried to Murder the Newborn Child" ([*JB* 3. 221]). The nephew's love causes his uncle to materialize, even as the boy's love for his father constructs the chariot that carries him to the other world (*RV* 10. 135). The poignancy of the boy's failure to embrace his beloved uncle—to hold his *body*—is an intensely human moment injected against the stream of an otherwise routine Brāhmaṇa passage, the purpose of which is to teach the "disembodying chant" by which one shakes off the body.

But the second half of the story takes another unconventional tack. Leaving his uncle, Keśin searches for a Brahmin to say the chant for him; though he knows it himself, he cannot perform the ritual, since he is a king and not a Brahmin. The man he finds is a stranger, scorned by the Brahmins of Keśin's family; he is a Brahmin, but an esoteric Brahmin. Like the beloved uncle, he is a man who straddles the worlds of the living and the dead; he is living among the corpses like a dead man, but he still has his "shadow"—the breath of life—the only part of the uncle that Keśin could see, and a substance that he could not embrace. This man, who is not even an uncle, let alone a father, nevertheless gives Keśin the gift that fathers often give sons in these texts: by completing the ritual that the uncle had begun, he frees Keśin from his body and therefore from his fear of death.

The meanings that emerge from our comparisons of the

Bhṛgu story with the *Ṛg Veda* and with other Brāhmaṇa texts do not, however, explain the particular point that it makes, distinct from all the other variants. To come closer to that point, we must pass beyond the manifest content—the discussion of the nature of the other world, the relationship between fathers and sons, and the necessity of performing sacrifices and preventative rites correctly—to the latent, symbolic content of the myth.

One immediate generalization that one can make about that symbolic content is that it is physically violent; terrible mutilations of the body occur in the other world. The text has a straightforward explanation for this violence, as we have seen: the *lex talionis*. But to the extent that the reversals in the other world are simply logical inversions, without moral implications, it remains for us to explain why the *Jaiminīya* chose to depict the inversions of violent acts, and acts of eating, rather than the inversion of other, less highly charged acts, both sacred and profane. So, too, the descriptions of sacrificial acts as a form of protection against inverted punishments in the other world belong to the layer of meanings with which the Brāhmaṇas are primarily concerned: the power of the violent sacrifice to render potential tragedy harmless. But to move beneath this level, we must ask why the *Jaiminīya* adopted this particular imagery: the images of people devouring one another, soundlessly screaming, while naked black men and beautiful women look on. To anyone familiar with the literature of dreams, the answer is not far to find: this is a dream landscape.

Bhṛgu's immediate reaction to the first scene is to ask "Has this happened?"—i.e., "Is it real, or is it a dream, a nightmare?" Similarly, the first words that Keśin Dārbhya says when he meets the ghost of his uncle are "Have I gone crazy?" The images in Bhṛgu's adventure are images that recur in dreams, Indian and non-Indian; they are the haunting images of dismemberment, forbidden foods, sexual temptation, and cannibalism. But the *Jaiminīya* tale is not the report of a dream; it is the record of a highly stylized recasting of a dream in the form of a story. Like all Brāhmaṇas, the *Jaiminīya* is committed to the happy ending: the son comes out unscathed— indeed, far stronger than before; for now he has learned to protect himself from the dangers he has seen. The other world turns out to be not a place from which one cannot escape but a nightmare from which one can awaken. It is a dream of a wish that is fulfilled: the wish to survive danger and win happiness. Yet the vision of the dangers of that world—and our fear that it might not, perhaps, be quite so easy for all of us to protect ourselves from them—sets the dominant tone of the story, lending it its air of threat if not of tragedy.

3
The Fear of God

The Vedic ritual provides an arena in which deep human fears can be transfigured and channeled into a formalized contest for knowledge. Underlying this formal contest is a more basic competition between fathers and sons, one that is acted out far more blatantly in many myths (including other *Jaiminīya* stories that we will soon encounter) than it is within the narrower formal constraints of the ritual. Most of the Brāhmaṇas control this competition (one can hardly call it a "controlled catastrophe," like the sacrificial slaughter itself) and defuse it; but when the *Jaiminīya* relates the story of the competition, it reinfuses it with the cruder base of the conflict, which it introduces in the form of folktales about the aggression of fathers against sons.

Stories of conflicts between fathers and sons may be seen on three levels in this text. First, there are battles on the highest cosmic level, the battles of gods and demons or of gods against men, in which there are no explicit references to fathers or sons, though such relationships may be implicit or assumed. Second, there are battles between gods and men in which the gods are explicitly identified as the fathers of the men. Finally, there are tales in which fathers, uncles, or priests attack young male children. Underlying all three levels is an implicit analogy that works in both directions: human fathers and sons call into play the powers of gods over men, but the stories about gods and demons (or men) often incorporate anthropomorphic details or incidents that betray a considerable preoccupation with emotional conflict among members of the human family.

Since the manifest focus of the *Jaiminīya* is theological, images of the family, like images of power and danger, are expressed primarily in terms of the liturgy. It may be that images of the human father underlie images of the divine father in all religions, as Freud and others have argued; but whether or not this is so, it is quite evident that the *Jaiminīya* takes as primary the image of the god and superimposes upon it the image of the father. (If one accepts the hypothesis that the father is the basis of the construction of the image of god, one would then say that the *Jaiminīya* brings out what was always implicit in the image of the god by making explicit the analogy between the god and the father.) In the tale of Bhṛgu, the father is the god Varuṇa, but in other tales of this genre ("The Son Who Was Better Than His Father," "The Ghost of the Beloved Uncle") the older male whom the boy encounters in the other world is a mortal father or uncle. Clearly, the fear of both gods and fathers is closely bound up with the fear of death. But to see the parallels between gods and fathers from the Indian point of view, we must begin with the *Jaiminīya* concept of god as a father and then proceed to its concept of the father as a god.

Although the majority of the Brāhmaṇas depict the relationship between gods and men as one of mutual nourishment, there are some passages—particularly in the *Jaiminīya*—that reveal a deep-seated jealousy and even hostility of the gods toward men (O'Flaherty 1976, pp. 78–93). This conflict, on the highest level, is clearly stated in the following tale.

The Gods Make Men Evil (*JB* 1. 97–98)

The gods and demons were striving against each other. The

gods created a thunderbolt, sharp as a razor, that was man [*puruṣa*]. They hurled this at the demons, and it scattered the demons, but then it turned back to the gods. The gods were afraid of it, and so they took it and broke it into three pieces. Then they saw that the divinities had entered into this man in the form of hymns. They said, "When this man has lived in the world with merit, he will follow us by means of sacrifices and good deeds and asceticism. Let us therefore act so that he will not follow us. Let us put evil in him." They put evil in him: sleep, laziness, anger, hunger, love of dice, desire for women. These are the evils that assail a man in this world.

Then they enjoined Agni [fire] in this world. "Agni, if anyone escapes evil and aspires to do good things in this world, try to ruin him." And they enjoined Vāyu [wind] in the intermediate air in the same way, and the sun in the sky. But Ugradeva Rājani said, "I will not harm mankind, though I have heard that these three high gods are inclined to harm mankind." And the gods do not harm the man who knows this, though they do try to destroy the man who tries to harm the man who knows this.

The gods of the three worlds unite to keep men out of heaven; they take away from men the hymns that are their source of divine strength, hymns that the gods use in their battles against their fraternal enemies, the demons. When the human pawn outlives its usefulness in the fraternal battle, the battle between fathers and sons takes precedence over the battle between brothers (O'Flaherty 1976, pp. 249–50).

But the battle between brothers may itself be expressed on the purely human level as well as in terms of the cosmic battle between the gods and their demonic older brothers. Familial conflicts in the Brāhmaṇas are always set against the broader backdrop of that archetypal sibling rivalry. But just as the image of the father works in both directions—suggesting the human aspects of the divine father as well as the divine aspects of the human father—so too the tales of cosmic brothers (gods and demons) and the tales of human brothers invite us to use what we know about each to help us understand the other. The fraternal conflict on an ostensibly human level is quite explicit in the following tale.

Trita and His Brothers (*JB* 1. 184)

Thirst overcame the Āptyas when they were in the forest, leading two gifts [cows]. They found a well. Now neither Ekata [the first of the three Āptya brothers] nor Dvita [the second] wanted to climb down, but Trita [the third brother] climbed down. When the two of them had drunk and were satiated, they covered him with a chariot wheel and went away with the cows. He wished, "Let me get out of here; let me have help." He saw this chant and praised with it. As he said the closing words, ". . . with drops," Parjanya [the god of rain] floated him upwards with rain; he floated him right up to the chariot wheel that had covered him. For that chant is one that gets you out and gets you help; he did indeed find a way out and find help. He followed their footsteps, and, as he came up to them, one of them became a bear and the other became a monkey, and they scampered away into the woods. And so this is also a chant for overcoming fraternal rivals, for he turned the two of them into a bear and a monkey when they were in fraternal rivalry against him.

If we look backwards for a source of this story, all we can find is a single verse in the *Ṛg Veda*: "When Trita was being kept in a well, he called to the gods for help; Bṛhaspati heard that and set him free from that tight spot" (*RV* 1. 105. 17). This is a situation that occurs quite often in the *Ṛg Veda*: a sage is trapped, and the gods set him free (cf. O'Flaherty 1981, pp. 16–17). Onto this base, perhaps inspired by the sage's name ("The Third"), the *Jaiminīya Brāhmaṇa* has grafted the tale of three brothers, a story that not only contains many well-known motifs from world folklore (as many of the *Jaiminīya* tales do) but is actually, in its entirety, a Stith Thompson Tale Type (number 654). Yet the *Jaiminīya* has added, characteristically, a touch of its own: the transformation of the two wicked brothers into a bear and a monkey. That this is peculiar to the *Jaiminīya* is further evident when we look sideways, to the only other version of the tale attested in the Brāhmaṇas, which tells the story much as the *Jaiminīya* does but omits the episode of the bear and the monkey (*ŚB*, cited by Sāyaṇa on *Ṛg Veda* 1. 105; cf. Oertel 1897, pp. 18–19, and *Lost Brāhmaṇas*, pp. 19–21). That episode is then greatly expanded in the *Mahābhārata* version of the story, which is altogether more detailed:

> [Vaiśampāyana said,] "While the noble Trita was living in a well, he drank Soma. His two brothers abandoned him and went home, and then Trita, that best of Brahmins, cursed them."
>
> [Janamejaya said,] "How did that great ascetic fall in, and how was he abandoned by his two brothers? How did his two brothers leave him in a well and go home? Tell me this, if you think I am fit to hear it."
>
> [Vaiśampāyana said,] There were in a former time three brothers who were sages, called Ekata, Dvita, and Trita [First, Second, and Third]. . . . Among them, Trita became most famous for his ritual acts and his studies; he was like his father. . . . Now, one day, Ekata and Dvita began thinking about doing a sacrifice in order to get rich. They got the idea of taking Trita and collecting animals that could be sacrificed. "And then," they thought, "we will drink Soma and enjoy the fruits of the sacrifice." And the three brothers did just this.
>
> When they had gathered the sacrificial animals, the great sages set out toward the East. Trita was going in front, quite cheerfully, and Ekata and Dvita were driving the animals behind. But when the two saw that great herd of animals, they got the idea, "How can we get these cows for just the two of us, without Trita?" Then the two plotted together, Ekata and Dvita, and this is the evil thing they agreed upon: "Trita

is so good at doing sacrifices and so well versed in the Vedas, he will easily get lots of other cows. So let us two go away together, driving the cows with us, and let Trita go wherever he likes, without us." But as the three of them were going along in the night, a wolf appeared on their path. Now there was a big well on the bank of the Sarasvatī River, not far away, and when Trita saw the wolf standing on the path in front of him, he ran away in terror of it and fell into that well, which was quite deep and terrifying to all creatures and altogether horrible.

When Trita was in the well, he began to wail in agony, and the two other sages heard him. But when his brothers, Ekata and Dvita, realized that he had fallen into a well, they went away and left him, out of fear of the wolf and also out of greed. And so that sage, who had such great ascetic powers, was abandoned by his two brothers, who were greedy for animals, and was left inside a well that had no water in it but was filled with dust and overgrown with grass and weeds. Trita felt that he was like a sinner who had plunged into hell, and he was afraid of dying because he had never drunk Soma. "But how," he wondered, "can I drink Soma when I am here?" As the wise man reflected upon this, he chanced to see a weed hanging down in the well. Then the sage imagined that there was water in that dust-choked well, and he imagined that there were fires for an oblation, and he imagined that that weed was the Soma plant, and he thought about the three kinds of hymns from the three Vedas. He made the gravel in the well into the pressing stones [for the Soma], and with them he pressed out the Soma; he made the water into butter and divided it into shares for the gods. Then he made a loud noise, which pierced heaven. . . . The gods came to him and accepted their shares, and, when they were pleased, they offered to give him whatever he wanted. The boon he chose was this: "Get me out of here! And let anyone who bathes in this well get what someone who has drunk Soma gets." Then the Sarasvatī rose up to that spot with her waves, and Trita

was cast up by her and stood there, honoring the gods. The gods went back where they had come from, and Trita went contentedly back to his own house.

But he was furious when he came upon his two brothers, the sages, and he spoke harshly to them and cursed them: "Since you were so greedy for animals that you abandoned me and ran away, therefore, because of that evil deed, you will become, by my curse, animals with sharp teeth, and your offspring will be cow-tailed monkeys and bears and monkeys." And as he said this, at that very moment that is what they became, because whatever he said came true. [*MBh* 9. 35. 3–7, 12, 14–35, 44–51]

This version of the story begins with a highly condensed summary that is very much like the Ṛg Vedic verse on which the tale is based. But then, in response to an audience request for further detail, the Epic bard spins a tale much longer than the *Jaiminīya* version, making all the moves explicit and painting in all the emotions that the *Jaiminīya* left to be inferred from the action. In addition, the *Mahābhārata* introduces a wolf and a curse to explain the presence of the bears and monkeys at the end, where the *Jaiminīya* merely implies that the brothers became physically transformed into the beasts that, spiritually, they had already become. Though each generation identifies the *deus ex machina* as a god of its own pantheon (Bṛhaspati in the *Ṛg Veda*, Parjanya in the *Jaiminīya*, and Sarasvatī [plus the gods in general] in the *Mahābhārata*), the Vedas remain the central power behind the story. Indeed, the *Mahābhārata* out-Vedas the Vedic texts when it has Trita not merely recite a Vedic verse but perform an entire imaginary Vedic sacrifice. This unbroken Vedic sacred thread connects the three versions of the story.

Thus the Brāhmaṇas cast the sacred drama with the dramatis personae of the nuclear family: the tales of gods and men become, explicitly, tales of fathers and sons—sons who are brothers. This drama is then gradually focused in the *Jaiminīya* on a particular conflict between a divine father and a human son or sons, a process that takes place in three stages, each of which is represented by extant tales in the *Jaiminīya*. First, the general categories of gods and men are narrowed; the result is a cycle of tales about a particular god—Indra in opposition to a particular human enemy, often an unwilling worshiper. In the second stage, this enemy is identified as Indra's son, Kutsa. And, finally, the conflict between a human father and son is presented without a theological frame, though such a frame may perhaps always be implicit.

On the first level, one of the most straightforward myths of resistance against Indra as an object of worship is this tale:

Indra and the Dolphin (*JB* 3. 193–94)

All creatures praised Indra, but Śarkara the dolphin [*śiśumāra*] did not wish to praise him. Indra said to him, "Praise me," but he replied, "I will not praise you. For I move about inside the ocean, under water, merely emerging [from time to time]. This is what I will praise you with," and he showed him the water. Then Indra used his rain and thunderclouds to drive the dolphin to swim upward onto dry land, and then he dried him up with a wind from the north. As the dolphin lay there all dried up, he realized, "Indra has brought me to this condition. All right, I will praise him, and perhaps when he is praised he will let me swim back into the ocean." He praised Indra and asked him to let him swim back into the ocean, and so Indra used his rain to put him back into the ocean. . . . Through this same hymn of praise, the dolphin went up into heaven and became a constellation there.

The parallel passage in the *Pañcaviṃśa* (*PB* 14. 5. 15) is pointless: a sage of the "Dolphin" school, named Śarkara, refused to praise Indra until Indra caused the water to recede from him (i.e., caused a drought, the usual measure taken by Indra to deal with impious mortals [O'Flaherty 1976, pp. 195–96, 291–302]). That the dolphin is a dolphin is essential to the reversal at the heart of the story: where Parjanya (a rain god, like Indra) *saved* the virtuous Trita by using floods of rain to remove him from a well, Indra *harms* the recalcitrant dolphin by using floods of rain to remove him from the water that is his element. The *Jaiminīya* takes the traditional motif of the drought used for theological blackmail (a motif also known to the Hebrew Bible, as in the story of Elijah) and transforms it into a highly vivid and original image: the playful dolphin, rebellious and blasphemous, scorns Indra by splashing water on him (probably with his tail, to add insult to injury, though perhaps just with his flippers); in the end, stranded and helpless, he knuckles under and is rewarded with heavenly status—the mandatory happy ending of the Brāhmaṇas.

Another tale of Indra in conflict with a worshiper begins with a simple episode, not unlike the story of the dolphin, but it then branches off into several apparently unrelated adventures.

Indra as the Ram of Medhātithi (*JB* 3. 234–36)

Medhātithi, as a householder, caused a sacrifice to be held for the Vibhindukīyas. Dṛḍhadyut Āgastya was the Udgātṛ priest, Gaurīviti was the Prastotṛ priest, Acyutacyut was the Pratihartṛ, Vasukṣaya was the Hotṛ, and Sanaka and Navaka, the sons of Kavi, were the two Adhvaryus. Medhātithi wanted cattle, Sanaka and Navaka wanted women, and each of the others had his own wish; for in the old days people used to perform sacrifices for various reasons. Now, when they had achieved their separate desires, they arose; but Indra took the form of a ram of Medhātithi and kept trying to drink their Soma. They kept throwing him out, saying, "Medhātithi's ram has come to drink our Soma." Then Indra took his own form and came to drink Soma there, and from that time on they summon Indra by calling him, "O ram of Medhātithi."

Now, when Medhātithi wanted cattle, he saw this chant and praised with it: "Shatterer of fortresses, young poet"

[*RV* 1. 11. 4] and he broke open the cow pen; then he broke open the cave with the verse "With your stones you opened the cave of the cow pen" [*RV* 1. 11. 5] The cattle came out. The ones that came out first were the cattle who are here now; after them came out cows with golden horns and two udders; and after them came out two heavenly nymphs [Apsarases] wearing golden robes. The householder [Medhātithi] set his heart on the two nymphs. "These two are mine," he said, "because they were won under my householdership." "No," said Sanaka and Navaka, "you did the sacrifice in order to get cattle. Those are your cattle. We are the ones who wanted women; those two are our women." While they were arguing about this, Medhātithi went for one of the two nymphs, but she pushed him away. She became the animal that has a kind of dewlap. The other one smiled, and she became a kind of small golden hind. . . . Then the cows with golden horns and two udders ran back to the place from which they had come out, for they thought, "This householder has done a dishonest thing. We will not belong to someone who does dishonest things." And to this day these have become the ferocious bulls of the Vibhinduka country who are known as motley-colored.

Now, Medhātithi and Triśoka, the two sons of Kaṇva, were rivals in sacred knowledge. They said, "Let us cross over a blazing fire." Now, when they crossed it, Triśoka crossed over right on top of it, but it scorched the eyelashes of Medhātithi. Then Triśoka said to his rival, "I have beaten you." "No you haven't," said Medhātithi, "for you are the son of a demon woman. The gods don't want you to touch them." Then they said, "Let us cross over water." They crossed the flowing Rathaspā River, and Triśoka crossed right over on top of it; but the two chariot wheels of Medhātithi got wet, for the river is called Rathaspā ("Chariot-wetting") because wheels do get wet in it. Then Triśoka said to his rival, "I have beaten you." "No you haven't," said Medhātithi, "for you are the son of a demon woman, and the gods don't want you to touch them."

"Come," they said, "let us liberate some cattle." Triśoka immediately let loose the hairless and earless cattle, who got hot and urinated and defecated, . . . and ran away to the West and entered the Sindhi River, where they became salt. . . . But Medhātithi, who still wanted cattle, sacrificed for a whole year and brought cattle out of a cave made of stone by saying the verse "With your stones you opened the cave of the cow pen."

Looking backwards, we can view this story as an expansion not only of the several Ṛg Vedic verses that it explicitly cites (verses addressed to Indra) but of another Ṛg Vedic verse that is not quoted in the story: "Indra became a ram and led away Kaṇva, the father of Medhātithi" (*RV* 8. 2. 40). In the *Jaiminīya* this verse is expanded: like the leopard that in Kafka's parable interrupts the sacrifice and eventually becomes part of the ceremony, the ram that they keep trying to push away, so that Indra will come to them, turns out to have been Indra himself all along.

The sexual notoriety of the ram then leads the *Jaiminīya* to append a second story about Medhātithi's cosacrificers, who wanted not cattle (the central thread of the Medhātithi story) but women, and who succeed in obtaining celestial nymphs. When, as a result of this episode, Medhātithi loses his cattle, the *Jaiminīya* starts in all over again to get them for him, and it uses this as an opportunity to tell the tale of another sort of supernatural woman, the demonic mother of Medhātithi's fraternal rival, Triśoka (the hero of the tale of "The Lover of the Demon's Daughter" [*JB* 3. 72–74].)

The competition between the sons of Kaṇva appears in a much milder form in the *Pañcaviṃśa*:

Vatsa and Medhātithi were both sons of Kaṇva. Medhātithi reproached Vatsa, saying, "You are not a Brahmin; you are the son of a Śūdra mother." Vatsa replied, "As an ordeal of truth [*ṛtena*], let us walk through fire, to decide which of the two of us is more of a Brahmin." With the Vatsa-chant,

Vatsa walked through the fire; with the Medhātithi-chant, Medhātithi walked through the fire. Not even a hair of Vatsa was burned by the fire, and that was precisely what he had wished for. For the Vatsa-chant is one that grants wishes. [*PB* 14. 6. 6]

The story makes perfectly good sense in this form: the bastard proves his true nobility, and, one assumes, Medhātithi has to acknowledge the superiority of his half-brother. When the episode of the competing brothers appears in the *Jaiminīya*, however, the half-brother is not merely half-caste but half-human, the ordeal is not merely an ordeal by fire but an ordeal by water as well, and the loser (the full brother) wins. The *Jaiminīya* never hesitates to make a good story better.

The three episodes in the *Jaiminīya* are only loosely connected. The *Śāṭyāyana*, which tells the story in almost the same words as the *Jaiminīya*, stops at the end of the first part ("From that time on, they summon Indra. . . ."), where a sensible narrative would stop, and where Venkaṭamādhava's commentary on *Ṛg Veda* 1. 51. 1 stops (*Lost Brāhmaṇas*, pp. 5–6). The subsequent episodes in the *Jaiminīya* are dragged in—by the hair, as it were—when Medhātithi keeps losing what he has gained. He loses the first set of cattle when he lusts after the nymphs and makes the wrong choice; his greed to have the women as well as the cattle is regarded as dishonest, and he loses both women and cattle. When he gets them back, he loses them again, by failing to match the demonic magic powers of Triśoka and by trying to pull rank and rely on his superior birth (the very factor that the *Pañcaviṃśa* version takes pains to prove invalid). As a result of this double-dealing, the cattle disperse and become salt. Finally, Medhātithi gets his cattle in the straightforward, traditional way: he sacrifices and says the Vedic verses. Before the tale reaches this anticlimactic, formulaic ending, however, the *Jaiminīya* wanders through a nonsacrificial world of nymphs and demonic women and contests in the performance of miracles.

Though Indra appears in the Medhātithi story as a ram, and

though it is a story with sexual ramifications, the relationship between Indra and Medhātithi gives no hint of a sexual competition. When the worshiper is a woman, however, Indra's aggression may take on sexual overtones, direct or indirect. Such an indirect approach may be seen in this tale:

Indra Dances for Upamā (*JB* 3. 245–48)

At the battle of the Ten Kings, Kṣatra ["Royal Power"], the son of Prātardana, was hemmed in. Kṣatra said to his domestic priest, Bharadvāja, "Sage, I take refuge with you. Find a way out for us here." Bharadvāja wished, "Let us win the battle," and he saw this chant and praised with it, saying, "Indra will come when we call, and we will win the battle."

Now, Upamā, the daughter of Savedas, was the wife of Kṣatra, and she was very beautiful. When her brother was killed in the battle, she was badly shaken, and, as she was running about, Indra set his heart on her. He put on a dried antelope hide and wore a shoulder yoke, with a basket holding a loaf of bread on one side and a basket of curds and butter on the other side. He went after her and began to dance near her. As he danced, he smeared her with melted butter; she kept pushing him away, but he danced again near her. Evening came, and they parted, and then her husband asked her, "Did you see anything today?" and she said, "Nothing but an old man who kept dancing near me. He had a shoulder yoke with a loaf of bread on one side and butter and curds on the other, and the more I pushed him away, the more he kept coming back and dancing near me."

Her husband said, "That was Indra, who came in answer to our call. Now we will win the battle. That was Indra! Don't insult him, but speak to him and make him your friend, saying, 'Let us win the battle.'" In the morning, they met again; he had the same shoulder yoke, and he began to dance. But now that she wished to touch him, he kept going farther away from her. Then she thought to herself, "I had better

talk to him," and she said, "What do you have in that basket?"

Indra replied, "A poisonous snake is in the basket for you." She said, "Little boy, if it is poisonous, my father will kill that wild animal." Indra said, "I love to look at your thing; let me touch it and stroke it with my hand." She replied, "How is it that you love my thing? How would you stroke it with your hand?" Indra said, "This way and that way. . . ."

Then she ran after him and said, "Let us win the battle." He shook his antelope hide and said, "Just as these [hairs] fall away in all directions, so let the enemies of Kṣatra run away in all directions from this place." As he said this, he scattered the hairs of the hide, and they became horse-drawn chariots, and with them Kṣatra won the battle. Then Bharadvāja said, "We have not fallen into the pit [*dāra*]," and because he said that, this chant is called the "nonpit" [*Adāra*] chant.

The conversation between Indra and Upamā (whose name means "simile") is composed almost entirely of similes, metaphors, and obscure allusions; the passage is corrupt in more ways than one, and my translation is highly speculative. Yet the general meaning of the story is clear enough. Indra offers Upamā sacred food that she at first rejects; he smears her with butter, an obvious and rather crude sexual metaphor but also a form of the sacrificial oblation of melted butter. Upamā uses the lust which she inspires in the immortal Indra to help her husband; but Indra also gets what he wants; for the erotic banter and the fact that the woman runs after him indicate that the woman succumbs to his blandishments, with the tacit consent of her pandering husband. The final etymology, which appears to be no more than the usual formula that defuses the story, has a double meaning that is ironic. *Adāra* does indeed refer to rescue from a pit. The *Jaiminīya* tells several tales of men who are rescued from pits, including, as we have seen, Trita; and in the *Ṛg Veda* the Aśvins rescue several people from pits, including men who are separated from their wives. Now, the word *dāra* means "wife" as well as "pit," and the *Adāra* chant in the tale of Upamā is more properly the chant of a man who does not have a wife—or, perhaps, a man whose wife has been stolen by a supernatural lover.

The man who is most famous in the *Ṛg Veda* for having been rescued by the Aśvins from a pit where he was kept from his wife is Cyavana (*RV* 1. 106. 6). In the Brāhmaṇas, Cyavana becomes a man who uses his wife to seduce divine lovers (the Aśvins) and thus to win power for himself, even as Kṣatra used Upamā to seduce Indra. In the *Jaiminīya*, moreover, Cyavana comes into conflict not only with the Aśvins but with Indra as well in a second episode, appended to the usual encounter with the Aśvins. The first encounter is described in this tale:

The Rejuvenation of Cyavana (*JB* 3. 120–29)

Cyavana, the son of Bhṛgu, said to his sons, "I know the Brāhmaṇa of the Vāstupa. Therefore put me down on the sacrificial place [*vāstu*] and go away on the thrice-returning departure." They said, "We cannot do that, for people will cry out against us and revile us, saying, 'They are abandoning their father.'" "No," he said, "by this means you will be better off, and by this I hope to become young again. Leave me and go forth." As he gave them this command, they placed him at the fountain of youth on the Sarasvatī River, and they went forth on the thrice-returning departure. As he was left behind, he wished, "Let me become young again, and find a young girl for a wife, and sacrifice with a thousand [cows]."

Cyavana saw this hymn and praised with it, and at that moment Śāryāta the Mānava [descendant of Manu] settled down with his clan near him. The young boys who were

cowherds and shepherds smeared Cyavana with mud and with balls of dust and cowshit and ashes. Cyavana then produced a condition among the Śāryātis so that no one recognized anyone else: a mother did not know her son, nor a son his mother. Śāryāta said [to his people], "Have you seen anything around here that could have caused this state of affairs?" They said to him, "Nothing but this: there is an old man on his last legs lying there. The boys who are cowherds and shepherds smeared him today with mud and balls of shit and dust and ashes. This has happened because of that."

Śāryāta said, "That was Cyavana, the son of Bhṛgu, who knows the Brāhmaṇa of the Vāstupa. His sons have left him in the sacrificial place and gone away." Then Śāryāta ran up to Cyavana and said, "Honor to you, great sage; have mercy, sir, on the Śāryātis." Now, Śāryāta had a beautiful daughter named Sukanyā ["Lovely Maiden"]. Cyavana said, "Give me Sukanyā." "No," said the king, "mention anything else of value." But Cyavana said, "No, I know the Brāhmaṇa of the Vāstupa. Put her down beside me today at evening, and go away with your clan." They said, "Let us discuss this, and then we will give you our answer." They held a council together and said, "We might obtain a few treasures with her, two or three at the most, but this way we will obtain everything with her. Hell, let's give her to him." They gave her to him, but they said to her, "My dear girl, this is a worn-out old man, who will not be able to run after you. As soon as we have harnessed the horses, run after us right away."

And so, when they had harnessed the horses, she stood up and was about to run after the clan, but Cyavana said, "Serpent, come and help your friend to save his life." And a black snake rose up right against her as she was about to go. When she saw it, she sat right down again.

The two Aśvins, who have no share in the Soma offerings, happened to be wandering about there. They came to Sukanyā and said, "My dear girl, this is an old man, not whole, not fit to be a husband. Be our wife." "No," she said, "I will be the wife of the man to whom my father gave me." Then they went away, but Cyavana had overheard them, and he said to Sukanyā, "My dear girl, what was all that noise about?" She said, "Two men—the handsomest men I have ever seen—came to me and said, 'My dear girl, this is an old man, not whole, not fit to be a husband. Be our wife.'" "And what did *you* say?" "'No,' said I, 'I will be the wife of the man to whom my father gave me.'"

Cyavana was very pleased about that. He told her, "Those were the two Aśvins; they will come tomorrow and speak to you in the same way. Now, you say to them, '*You* are the ones who are not whole; for though you are gods, you do not drink the Soma.' Then they will ask you, 'Who can see to it that we may share in the Soma?' 'My husband,' you say. This is my hope of becoming young again."

The next day, the two Aśvins came and said the same thing, and she said, "You are not whole; for though you are gods, you do not drink the Soma. My husband is whole, for he drinks the Soma." They said, "Who can see to it that we may share in the Soma?" "My husband," said she. Then they said to him, "Sage, sir, make us share the Soma." "All right," said he, "and you make me young again." They drew him down into the fountain of youth of the Sarasvatī River.

He said, "My dear girl, we will all come out looking the same; by this sign, you will know me." They did all come out looking the same, the handsomest men in the world; but she recognized him and could tell them apart. "This is my husband," she said, and they said to him, "Sage, we have granted your desire: you have become young again. Now teach us so that we may share the Soma." And he sent them to Dadhyañc.

Now, Indra had threatened to cut off the head of Dadhyañc if he told anyone the secret of the sacrifice: how the sacrifice is made whole when the head is cut off. The Aśvins gave Dadhyañc the head of a horse, through which he told

them the secret of the sacrifice. Indra cut off that head, and then the Aśvins replaced Dadhyañc's head. Thus the Aśvins became sharers in the Soma.

The central episode, the rejuvenation of Cyavana by the Aśvins, is framed by two brief sacrificial tales that extol the powers of the Brāhmaṇa of the Vāstupa and the horse sacrifice. The *Śatapatha Brāhmaṇa*, which is the only other Brāhmaṇa to tell the story of Cyavana in any detail, substitutes for the first episode (which is apparently unique to the *Jaiminīya*) a single sentence: "When the Bhṛgus, or the Angirases, reached the world of heaven, Cyavana, the son of Bhṛgu, was left behind, worn out and like a witch" (*ŚPB* 4. 1. 5. 1–15). How does this differ from the *Jaiminīya* version? In the first place, it is far briefer than the *Jaiminīya*. Moreover, a conflict that appears in the *Jaiminīya* in family terms (father versus sons) and in highly emotional and conversational terms appears here in an abstract form that is part of another common Brāhmaṇa formula: when all the sages reached heaven, one was left behind. In other words, the cosmic dimension of the *Śatapatha* (the journey to heaven) is translated in the *Jaiminīya* into a family dimension (the departure of the sons from home). As we analyze the *Jaiminīya* treatment of the Cyavana story, it will be interesting to continue to glance sideways at the parallels in the *Śatapatha*.

In the episode of the conflict with Śāryāta, where the *Jaiminīya* has the boys pelt Cyavana with cowshit and ashes, the *Śatapatha* speaks only of "clods of dirt." And where the "nonrecognition" that results from Cyavana's curse is, in the *Jaiminīya*, the nonrecognition of sons by mothers, the *Śatapatha* says that "fathers fought with sons, and brothers with brothers." Elsewhere in the *Jaiminīya*, in the tale "Kutsa Seduces Indra's Wife" (*JB* 3. 199–200), mothers who fail to recognize their sons sleep with them. For this highly charged situation, the *Śatapatha* substitutes the more usual, though still conflict-laden, encounter between male members of the nuclear family. Thus the *Jaiminīya* highlights the female and sexual aspects of the episode, the *Śatapatha* the male and martial aspects.

The characters of Cyavana and of Sukanyā emerge clearly from the next episode of the *Jaiminīya* text. Cyavana is a dirty old man, in possession of magical phallic powers, as is demonstrated by the big black snake that so stuns Sukanyā and makes her stay with him—a snake that does not appear in the *Śatapatha* version. The Śaryātis greatly underrate Cyavana and have no intention of giving their princess to him, but he wins her despite their plots and their hope of cheating him of his treasures. The *Śatapatha* (and the closely related *Śāṭyāyaṇa* fragment, cited by Venkaṭamādhava on *Ṛg Veda* 1. 116. 10 [*Lost Brāhmaṇas* 25–29]) omits the passages that give the story all of its humor and much of its meaning: Śāryāta's deliberations and realizations of the cause of his misfortunes; the conversation in which Cyavana asks for the girl; the episode in which Sukanyā is advised to run away; and her detailed explanation to the Aśvins of their inadequacy. The *Śatapatha* also omits the entire episode of recognition at the end, an episode that balances the curse of recognition at the beginning.

The tale of Cyavana may be seen as a conflict between fathers and sons on various levels. Cyavana is the son of Bhṛgu, the boy who competed with his own father—the god Varuṇa—in attempting to avoid the dangers of the other world. Cyavana, in his turn, is mocked for his old age by the young boys in Śāryāta's camp, and his revenge is to get back his own youth. And Cyavana does stave off death, at least for a while, by overcoming old age. That Cyavana is asserting his powers as a man in competition with younger men is symbolized by the rising of the black snake when Sukanyā tries to run away. But the competition in the other direction—Cyavana's competition with his own divine father—is developed not in this episode but in one that the *Jaiminīya* tells (though the *Śatapatha* does not) in a passage separate from the episode with the Aśvins and Sukanyā. This is a story in which Cyavana competes not with the Aśvins but with Indra himself, and he competes not for his own youth but for the Aśvins' right to the Soma.

Vidanvan and the Demon of Intoxication (*JB* 3. 159–61)

Śaryāta [*sic*], the son of Manu, performed a sacrifice in which gods and men drank the Soma together; that was the last time they drank the Soma together. In this sacrifice, Cyavana, the son of Bhṛgu, took a draught [of Soma] for the two Aśvins. Indra seized the cup and said, "What unknown cup is this?" Vidanvan, [another] son of Bhṛgu, struck back at Indra, saying, "Who dares to question the cup that this seer is presenting?" Then the gods got angry, and the sages got angry. The Maruts stood with spears in their hands, saying, "Now we will tear everything up; now he [*sic*; Indra?] will crush everything." But the sages summoned up the demon of Intoxication [Mada], whose head pierced the sky, and he attacked [Indra]. Then a great battle arose, and Agni advised Indra, "Let your anger dissolve; they are better than we are. If anyone makes them get angry, there will be nothing left here, for we [the gods] are born from them [the sages]." In this way, Agni calmed down Indra, who let go of his anger and fled with the gods.

But, after this, the sacrifice of these sages had no Indra and no gods. The sages wished out loud: "Let our sacrifice have Indra and the gods." Vidanvan, the son of Bhṛgu, saw these chants and praised with them. He summoned Indra with them and averted Indra's anger with them. Then Indra came to the sages' sacrifice and did not go away from them. Even now, the [male] sacrificial animals are called Vidanvan, and the [female] Vedic verses are called Vidanvan. They put this chant of Vidanvan to these verses as one would put a bull [to a cow], for pairing and begetting.

But the demon of Intoxication became frightened and said, "Do not summon me in vain; put me [somewhere]." They thought, "Let's drink [him]," and they said, "Let us bring

the wine that is the sap of Varuṇa; for no one was ever hurt by wine; wine is no killer." And so Intoxication, the demon, was placed in wine.

When gods and men are no longer together and no longer drink the Soma together, the two brothers (Cyavana and Vidanvan) side together against their celestial father, Indra. The gods go on strike; and though the sages get the upper hand by force (the demon of Intoxication), they nevertheless want the gods to be their friends. That Indra, a perennial drunkard, should be faced down by the demon drink is both fitting and ironic. It is a stroke of originality that is typical of the *Jaiminīya* in its humor, violence, and bathos.

The *Mahābhārata* directly juxtaposes the two incidents and further embroiders the *Jaiminīya* version of the tale of Cyavana. The text is too long for me to translate here word for word, but I will summarize the main points:

Cyavana, the son of Bhṛgu, performed asceticism in the same place for many years until an anthill grew over him. One day a king named Śaryāti [*sic*] came to that place with four thousand women and his beautiful daughter, Sukanyā. She came upon the anthill of Cyavana, and the sage fell in love with her. He spoke to her, but his throat was so dried up that she did not hear him. Then she saw his eyes shining out of the anthill and wondered, "What is this?" Curious, she pricked the eyes with a thorn. The irascible old sage became furious when his eyes were pierced, and he stopped up the shit and piss of the army of Śaryāti. When the king discovered that his army was suffering from this impediment, he asked everyone if they knew if someone had insulted the quick-tempered Cyavana, but no one knew of any such offense. Then Sukanyā said, "When I was wandering about, I saw something alive, shining out of an anthill. I thought it was some sort of firefly, and I pierced it."

When Śaryāti heard this, he went quickly to the anthill and folded his hands before the old sage and said, "Forgive what

the girl did in her ignorance and innocence." Then Cyavana replied to the king, "Your daughter is very beautiful, but she has fallen prey to greed and confusion. If I marry her, I will forgive her." When the king heard this, he gave his daughter to Cyavana. When Cyavana had married the girl, he relented, and the king and his army turned back.

After some time, the two Aśvins saw Sukanyā when she had bathed and was naked. They ran up to her and said, "Whose are you, and what are you doing in the forest? You have magnificent thighs." Sukanyā covered herself up and told them that she was the daughter of Śaryāti and the possession and wife of Cyavana. The Aśvins burst out laughing and said, "How could your father have given such a beautiful girl to an old man beyond the pleasures of sex? Get rid of Cyavana and choose one of us for your husband. Don't waste your youth!" Sukanyā replied, "I am satisfied by Cyavana, my husband." The [two] Aśvins said, "Then we will make your husband young and handsome, and you can choose a husband from the three of us. Tell your husband about this agreement."

Sukanyā did as they had told her and spoke to Cyavana. When he heard about it, Cyavana said, "Do it!" And so she said to the Aśvins, "Do it!" The Aśvins said, "Your husband must enter the water," and Cyavana, who wanted very much to be handsome, jumped into the water. The Aśvins jumped in, too; and then they all came out, all young and spectacularly handsome, indistinguishable from one another. But Sukanyā chose her own husband. Then Cyavana, who now had both his bride and his youth and good looks, spoke in joy to the Aśvins: "Because you have given me, an old man, youth and good looks, and this woman is my wife, I will let you drink the Soma before the very eyes of Indra, the king of the gods." When the Aśvins heard this, they went happily back to heaven, and Cyavana and Sukanyā made love like a god and a goddess.

Now, when Śaryāti heard that Cyavana had become young again, he went joyously to Cyavana's hermitage, taking his

army with him. Then Cyavana celebrated a sacrifice for King Śaryāti, and at that sacrifice he drew a cup of Soma for the Aśvins. But Indra seized the Soma of the Aśvins and said, "I don't think these two Aśvins are fit for the Soma." Still, Cyavana continued to pour Soma for the Aśvins; but when Indra hurled his thunderbolt at Cyavana, Cyavana paralyzed Indra's arm. And then Cyavana offered into the fire an oblation intended to injure the god, and by the power of the sage's asceticism there arose a Fury named Intoxication, a demon whose great body neither gods nor demons could control. Licking his lips, he ran at Indra to eat him.

When Indra saw Intoxication coming to eat him, he started licking his lips in terror (his arm was still paralyzed), and he said, "From now on, Cyavana, the two Aśvins are fit for the Soma." When Cyavana heard Indra's words, his anger subsided, and he set Indra free. Then the powerful sage dispersed Intoxication among drinking, women, dice, and hunting, in which it is reborn again and again. And when he had taken care of Intoxication and satisfied Indra with a drop of Soma (and given some to the gods, who had now been joined by the Aśvins), and had completed his sacrifice for King Śaryāti, Cyavana went back to his pleasures with the passionate Sukanyā in the forest. [*MBh* 3. 122. 1–27; 1. 123. 1–23; 1. 124. 1–24; 1. 125. 1–10]

Aside from the many small human details that the *Mahābhārata* has added, we can discern several basic changes. Cyavana's complex curse on the army of Śaryāti has now been changed to a bit of music-hall obscenity: the soldiers are all constipated (perhaps as an appropriate revenge for the shit with which Cyavana was pelted in the *Jaiminīya*—though not in the *Mahābhārata*—version of the tale). Sukanyā takes a far more active part in the story (it is she, not a group of anonymous naughty boys, who offends Cyavana), and Cyavana takes a far less active part: instead of devising the entire plan of rejuvenation, he merely responds to the Aśvins' suggestion. Intoxication, which in the *Jaiminīya* is put only into wine, is here distributed in a more complex way; yet this theme is also derived from the *Jaiminīya*, from the tale "The Gods Make Men Evil" (*JB* 1. 97) where dice and women (as in the *Mahābhārata*), as well as sleep, laziness, anger, and hunger, are involved. By the time of the Epic, Indra had lost his Vedic status and could no longer injure the sages merely by staying away; now he attacks them and must be literally paralyzed and terrorized.

Yet the basic distribution of power remains that of the *Jaiminīya*: gods and men are opposed, but men have the upper hand because they control the sacrifice. And so, even here, when men are so vitally endangered by the overt hostility of the powers-that-be, there is a happy ending. Though gods are intrinsically more powerful than men, the knowledge of the sacrifice turns the tables, and man wins out in the end.

4
The Fear of the Father

The conflict between father and son that is so brutally direct when the parent is a god becomes far more veiled and distorted when all the protagonists are human, though here, too, the victim always survives the father's attack. In many of these stories, the older man who tries to harm the child is not the father at all but an uncle or a priest. Indra's position along this spectrum is somewhat ambiguous. In the *Ṛg Veda,* Indra is regarded metaphorically as the father of men, but he is also said to be the biological father of certain particular men. In one hymn, Indra competes with an unnamed son when that son refuses to give him a share in the sacrifice—i.e., when the man refuses to worship him (*RV* 10. 28; O'Flaherty 1981, pp. 146–48). The *Jaiminīya* goes on to tell three tales about Indra as a biological father in conflict with his son on both the sexual and the ritual level. The fight begins in the first tale:

Kutsa Straps Down Indra's Balls (*JB* 1. 228)

Kutsa and Luśa summoned Indra in rivalry. Indra came to Kutsa's offering, but Kutsa bound him with a hundred straps on his two balls. Luśa said to Indra, "I have heard of you, O Bull, as one who has his own way, who binds [others] and urges on the sluggish. Come, free yourself from Kutsa and

come here. Why should someone like you remain bound by the two testicles?" [*RV* 10. 38. 5]. Indra broke all the straps apart and ran toward Luśa, but Kutsa called after him, "O Indra, here is the pressed Soma" [*SV* 1. 381]. Indra turned back to Kutsa, but Luśa called out to him, "Indra, come here, I invite you." Indra stood between the two. Then he said to them both, "Let each of the two of you take a part. I will drink with one of you by means of my self, and with the other by means of my greatness." They agreed to this, and each took a part: Kutsa won the self, and Luśa won the greatness.

In the Indian view the son is made out of the father's self, or actually is that self, and is therefore essentially indistinguishable from him (O'Flaherty 1980a, pp. 105–6). Since, as the Upaniṣads maintain, the self (or soul, *ātman*) of man is identical with the self (or godhead, *brahman*) of God, this is both a theological and psychological identity. The self that Kutsa wins is the quality that makes the father the same as the son; he wins Indra as a father. Luśa, by what is apparently default, wins Indra as protector, as one whose power or greatness he shares. Despite Indra's initial preference for Kutsa, and despite his final favor to him over Luśa, Kutsa's sexual aggression toward Indra—manifest here in his direct attack on Indra's balls—continues to assert itself:

Kutsa Seduces Indra's Wife (*JB* 3. 199–200)

Kutsa Aurava ["Thigh-born"] was made out of the two thighs of Indra. Just as Indra was, so was he, precisely as one would be who is made out of his own self. Indra made him his charioteer. He caught him with his wife, Śacī the daughter of Puloman, and when he asked her, "How could you do this?" she replied, "I could not tell the two of you apart." Indra said, "I will make him bald, and then you will be able to tell the two of us apart." He made him bald, but Kutsa bound a turban around his head and went to her. This is the

turban that charioteers wear. Indra caught him again [with his wife] and said to her, "How could you do this?" She said, "I still couldn't tell the difference, because he bound a turban around his head and then came to me." "I will smear dirt between his shoulders, and then you will be able to tell the difference between us." He did smear dirt between his shoulders—and so charioteers have dirt between their shoulders—but Kutsa covered it up and went to her. Indra caught them again and said, "How could you do this?" and again she said, "I still could not tell the two of you apart, for he covered up his upper torso and came to me." Then Indra bound Kutsa and said, "Now you are a wrestler [Malla]." Kutsa said, "Generous one, do not ruin us. Give us something that we can live on, for truly we were born from you." Indra said, "Shake the dirt off from between your shoulders." Kutsa shook it off, and it became the Rajas and Rajīyas, a great people.

Mingled in with some arcane etiologies (the origins of certain customs among charioteers and false folk etymologies of the names of the Rajas [from *rajas,* dust] and Mallas [from *mala,* dirt]) is a tale of overt sexual competition between father and son. That Kutsa and Indra are so much alike that a woman cannot tell them apart is an idea that begins in the *Ṛg Veda* (4. 1. 10), where, as we saw in the first Kutsa episode, it is also said that Kutsa bound Indra by the testicles. The *Jaiminīya* combines these concepts and goes on to tell a third tale of conflict between Kutsa and Indra, taking up the thread at the point where Kutsa is made into a king:

Indra Revives the Son of Kutsa's Enemy (*JB* 3. 200–202)

Upagu, the son of Suśravas, was the domestic priest [Purohita] of Kutsa. Kutsa said, "Let no one sacrifice. If anyone in my kingdom sacrifices, he will be stripped of all his possesssions. The gods do not eat anything that is not offered as an oblation; do not offer even the leaf of a tree as an oblation."

Now, Indra went to Upagu and said, "Please perform a sacrifice for me." But Upagu replied, "They do not offer sacrifice here; if anyone sacrifices, he will be stripped of all his possessions." Indra showed Upagu world after world, promising him, "If you perform the sacrifice, you will win this world." Then Upagu reflected, "Let them take away all my possessions. To hell with it; I will do the sacrifice." He said to Indra, "Let me sacrifice for you," and he performed the sacrifice. The butter offerings sprang up right away, and the Soma pressed itself in the mortars and pestles. Then he said to Indra, "Hide from Kutsa, far away." But Indra went right up to Kutsa, and Kutsa said to him, "Whom did you get to sacrifice for you?" "Upagu." Then Kutsa confiscated all of Upagu's property.

They took away all of his property. This happened a second and a third time. . . . The second time, they took away all of his property. The third time, Kutsa himself tore Upagu into pieces and scattered them in the water. When Suśravas, the son of Sthūra, found out that Kutsa Aurava had hacked his son into pieces and scattered them into the water, he ran to Kutsa and said, "Where have you put my son?" "He lies where he was scattered in the water." Suśravas went after him, and Indra took the form of a fish [*rohita*] and drank Soma from Suśravas's mouth. Then Suśravas realized, "This must be Indra. I will praise him. Then he will bring this man out of the water for me and revive him." He saw this chant and praised with it: "Indra, whose lips are fine for drinking, has drunk the powerful sacrificial drink, the drops mixed with barley" [*RV* 8. 92. 4]. Then Indra said to Suśravas, "With what desire are you praising me?" "Bring my son back to life." With the phrase, "Churn him out!" Indra churned him up out of the water, and then he brought him to life.

Here, instead of harming Indra, Kutsa harms Upagu, Indra's ally. Indra revives Upagu by "churning" him out of the water; but Kutsa was born when he was "churned" out of

Indra's thigh, as is indicated by his surname, "Aurava," which means "churned out of a thigh." Thus Upagu replaces Kutsa as Indra's son. Yet Indra does not make friends with this son; on the contrary, Indra's blatant refusal to take Upagu's very good advice about lying low leads directly to Upagu's death. (Indra is even more brazen in the *Pañcaviṃśa* variant of this episode: he holds the sacrificial cake in his hands and goes right up to Kutsa and says, "They have offered a sacrifice to me. Now what has become of your curse?" [*PB* 14. 6. 8].) Indra may be hungry—as he explicitly admits in this text—but more than anything else he wants to prove that he is more powerful than Kutsa. The betrayal of Upagu is merely an unfortunate side effect of Indra's central purpose, which is to outface Kutsa.

In the tale of Kutsa and Upagu, the final conflict centers on the killing and revival of a child. In another tale of this type the father fails to revive his son:

Vasiṣṭha's Dying Son and the Half-Verse (*JB* 2. 392)

The men of King Sudās threw Śakti, the son of Vasiṣṭha, into the fire. As they threw him in, Śakti said, "Indra! Bring us strength, as a father to his sons" [*RV* 7. 32. 26ab]. He was able to say only that much of the hymn when they threw him into the fire. Then Vasiṣṭha came and said, "What did my son say as he was being thrown into the fire?" They told him, "He was able to say only that much of the hymn—'Indra! Bring us strength, as a father to his sons'—and then they threw him into the fire." Vasiṣṭha said, "If my son had gotten to the last half of the verse—'Help us, O much-invoked Indra, in this ritual; let us, alive, find the light' [*RV* 7. 32. 26cd]—they would not have thrown him into the fire, and he would have lived out his whole life-span. He has run away to the god who is closest to the Kurus. Sacrificers who sing my son's verse will prosper."

This story is evidently constructed around the Ṛg Vedic

verse in which Indra is explicitly likened to a father coming to help a son. In the Brāhmaṇa story, the son's human father—a famous priest—comes to him; but without the presence of Indra (which was essential to the revival of Upagu's son) the human father can do nothing. Indeed, Vasiṣṭha seems to take smug satisfaction in his son's failure to complete the verse (and, by contrast, to exult in his own superiority as a Vedic chanter), though he also consoles himself with the faith that his son has reached the gods and has, moreover, established a chant that will keep his name alive in generations to come. There is, therefore, a happy ending in formulaic *Jaiminīya* terms, even from the standpoint of the dead son.

In most of the *Jaiminīya* tales, however, the child is actually revived. In one, the aggression of the older man is far more explicit, though here, perhaps by way of compensation, the man is not the child's father but merely an uncle.

THE UNCLE WHO TRIED TO MURDER THE NEWBORN CHILD (*JB* 3. 221)

When Vyaśva, the son of Sākamaśva, was still in the womb, his paternal uncle, Gaya, realized that he would be a great sage as soon as he was born. When he was born, Gaya ordered them to throw him out and to say that he was born dead. But the child's shadow did not leave him, and his own two thumbs gave him milk. Then they told Gaya, "The little boy that you ordered us to throw out is still alive." Gaya took his club and went out to kill the child. But Vyaśva prayed, "Let me get out of this; let me find help and a way out." He saw this chant and sang it over Gaya, and so Gaya's club fell backwards and split open his own head.

The symbolism of this episode is obvious. The theme of the slaughter of the innocents appears here in all of its power. The child is nursed not by an animal (as usually happens in stories of the birth of the hero) but by a strange foster mother of his own making: his two thumbs, which elsewhere serve as breast surrogates for abandoned boys (as in the *Mahābhārata* story of Māndhātṛ). Gaya's club, with which he intends to kill the child and which, instead, by the child's power, splits open Gaya's own head, is a symbol of the threatened and threatening paternal phallus. The child's shadow is both his vital sign and his symbolic stepmother.

In still another story, the child who is revived is no relation of the man who revives him. Here, as in the story of Gaya and Vyaśva, there is a simple happy ending.

The Sick Boy in the Ditch (*JB* 1. 151)

Anyone who wishes to live out a long life-span should recite the Purumīḍha chant. Now, Taranta and Purumīḍha were the sons of Vidadaśva and Mahī; their mother was Mahī, the daughter of Arcānanas. As they were traveling, a woman came to them and said, "My son is suffering from fever; cure him for me." They became rather angry and said, "How can someone talk to us like this?" [Then they said to her,] "Throw him in a ditch." The woman had faith in what she was told by men she thought of as "two sages of the gods, makers of mantras," and so she laid the boy in a ditch. When the two of them came back again, she went up to them and said, "The little boy whom you told me to throw into a ditch—he is still lying there in the hole where I put him." Then the two of them thought, "We have done something that is not very nice." And they prayed, "Let us get out of this, let us find something that will help us get away, let this little boy live." Then Purumīḍha saw this chant and he praised with it, and he asked, "What is the little boy's name?" "His name is Sudīti," [she answered]. Then Purumīḍha rubbed the boy, saying, "Let Agni come and protect Sudīti." And the boy came out of the ditch in that very condition [i.e., dead], but by the final word he came to life.

Into this tale, dealing with the power of the chant to bring the dead back to life, the *Jaiminīya* has introduced two interesting women. The first is the mother of the two sages, a woman who appears both in their matronymic (an unusual form of a name to be cited in the Brāhmaṇas) and in a phrase devoted to her own lineage. The second woman is the anonymous mother of the sick child, a woman whose literal-minded faith is both the source of a joke (for when they tell her to throw the boy in a ditch they are telling her to go to hell) and a touching demonstration of hope, born of desperation, that moves the arrogant young sages to pity and shame.

The *Jaiminīya* also builds a woman into another tale in which kings and priests come into conflict over a dead child:

THE CHARIOTEER AND THE VANISHING FIRE (*JB* 3. 94–96)

Vṛśa, the son of Jana, was the domestic priest [Purohita] of King Triyaruṇa, son of Trivṛśan of the Ikṣvākus. Now in the old days the domestic priest would hold the reins in the chariot for the king in order to watch out for the king, so that he would not do any harm. As the two of them [Vṛśa and Triyaruṇa] were driving along, they cut down with the wheel of the chariot the son of a Brahmin, a little boy playing in the road. One of the two [the king] had driven the horses forward, while the other [the priest] had tried to pull them to one side, but they came on so hard that he could not pull them aside. And so they had cut down the boy. They argued with each other about it: "You are the one who murdered him." "No, you are the one who murdered him." Vṛśa threw down the reins, stepped down from the chariot, and said, "*You* are the murderer." "No," said the king, "the one who holds the reins is the driver of the chariot. You are the murderer." "No," said the priest, "I tried to pull back to avoid him, but you drove the horses on. You are the murderer."

Finally they said, "Let us ask," and they went to ask the Ikṣvākus. The Ikṣvākus said, "The one who holds the reins is the driver. You are the murderer," and they accused Vṛśa the priest. He prayed, "Let me get out of this; let me find help and a way out. Let that boy come to life." He saw this chant

and brought the boy to life with it, saying, "For your skill, which brings the sap of life—" [*RV* 9. 65. 28a]. Now, the "sap of life" is the life's breath; and so with this verse he put the life's breath back in the child. And he continued, "—and for the chariot-horse, which is the drink—the lovely, much-desired, enlivening, enriching, inspiring drink—we pray to-day" [*RV* 9. 65. 28bc, 9. 65. 29abc). Now, the "drink" is the man; and so with this verse he revived him. For this is a chant that cures and makes restoration. And it is also a chant that gives you what you want. Whoever praises with this chant gets whatever he wants.

But Vṛśa was angry, and he went to Jana [his father] and said, "They gave a false and prejudiced judgment against me." Then the power went out of the fire of the Ikṣvākus: if they placed food on the fire in the evening, by morning it still had not been cooked; and if they placed food on the fire in the morning, the same thing happened to it [by evening]. Then they said, "We have displeased a Brahmin and treated him with dishonor. That is why the power has gone out of our fire. Let us invite him back." They invited him, and he came back, just like a Brahmin summoned by a king. As he arrived, he prayed, "Let me see this power of the fire." He saw this chant and sang it over the fire. Then he saw this: "The wife of Triyaruṇa is a flesh-eating ghoul [Piśācī]. She is the one who has covered the fire with a cushion and sits on it." Then he spoke these verses [from the *Ṛg Veda*]: "The young mother secretly keeps the boy tightly swathed and does not give him to the father. The people no longer see before them his altered face, hidden by the charioteer. Who is the boy that you are carrying, young woman? The chief queen, not the stepmother, gave him birth, for the embryo grew for many autumns. I saw him born when his mother bore him. Agni shines forth with a high light; by his power he makes all things manifest. He overpowers the godless forces of evil magic; he sharpens his two horns to gore the demons. Let Agni's bellowings reach to heaven as piercing weapons to destroy the demons. His angry glare breaks forth in ecstasy of

Soma. The obstacles of the godless cannot hold him back" [*RV* 5. 2. 1–2; 5. 2. 9–10].

As Vṛśa finished saying these verses, the power of the fire ran up into her and burnt her all up. Then they dispersed that power of the fire properly, here and there [in each house], and the fire cooked for them properly.

There are two closely related stories here. The first ends (with the usual formulaic flourishes) when the priest succeeds in reviving the dead child. This is a simple episode, making much the same point that was made in the tale of the sick boy in the ditch; and, like the story of "Vasiṣṭha's Dying Son and the Half-Verse," it is loosely based on a Ṛg Vedic verse. The equine theme of that verse (in which the "drink"—the ambrosial Soma—is likened to a horse) may have generated the idea for the lively argument between the king and his charioteer. The charioteer also appears in another Ṛg Vedic hymn, however, and that hymn is the basis of the second half of the story.

The second half takes up the theme of father and son in a powerful though obscure form. In the first half, there is no evidence that the dead boy was the son of the priest, as he is in the tale of Vasiṣṭha (though in one variant of the story, as retold in the *Bṛhaddevatā,* the dead boy is said to be the son of the Purohita, Vṛśa himself [Sieg 1902, p. 68], and even in the *Jaiminīya* he is the son of a Brahmin and hence is related, at least by caste, to Vṛśa, in opposition to the royal Triyaruṇa). In the second half, however, Vṛśa first seeks help from his own father and then, with that help, reveals a family conflict in which another "son"—the newborn fire, incarnate—is endangered. It is not clear from the Vedic verse whether this danger comes from the charioteer (from whom the child's mother is protecting him) or from the mother herself; but in the *Jaiminīya* it is unequivocally the mother, the demonic wife of Triyaruṇa.

Thus the *Jaiminīya* builds out of the enigmatic hints of the Ṛg Vedic verses a classical fairy tale with lurid sexual imagery:

a flesh-eating ogress has hidden her fiery child in a cushion, which she sits on; she is destroyed when the fire comes out of the cushion, enters her through her lap, and burns her to death. The *Jaiminīya* goes on to domesticate the story (the sexual fire is neatly divided up and set to work cooking properly), but the blunt images remain "unflattened" in memory. Several later texts retell this story, but none includes the fitting punishment of the queen, whose point of vulnerability is also the source of her threatening power. The deeper, nightmare threat of women is expressed only in the one image of the fire between her legs. Explicitly, the only danger that she poses is the danger to the sacrifice—the danger to the fire, which is needed to cook not only the sacred oblations but all profane food. These two types of cooking belong to the wife as well as to the domestic fire; it is she who cooks the everyday meals and makes it possible (by her mere presence at the ritual) for her husband to offer the oblations. But the sexual fire is the indirect sign of the demoness, who directly threatens the sacrificer, not by rendering him impotent, but by rendering impotent the sacrificial fire and hence the sacrifice itself.

5
The Fear of Wives

Women threaten the sacrifice in two ways in the Brāhmaṇas: evil women (demonesses) threaten to destroy the sacrifice (and the sacrificer), while good women (wives) pose a danger to the sacrificer through the likelihood that they will be seduced. For the sacrificer had to be a married man, and his wife was essential to his ritual completeness. In chapter six we will examine the negative, evil side of the ambivalent woman in the *Jaiminīya*, the demoness; first let us examine her positive, good side, her role as wife—a role that turns out to be ambivalent enough in itself.

One of the ways in which the *Jaiminīya* enlivens the stories that it shares with other Brāhmaṇas is by introducing new female characters or by expanding the role of the women who are already present in the stories.The women we have encountered so far are sometimes seductive (Upamā, Sukanyā, Indra's wife, the nymphs in Bhṛgu's final world) and sometimes dangerous (the wife of Triyaruṇa, and the two nymphs encountered by Medhātithi). There is a cycle of stories in the *Jaiminīya* in which a woman who plays a key role is both seductive and potentially dangerous by virtue of that seductiveness. Her own ambivalence is enhanced by the ambivalence of the man whom she betrays: when he is the hero, she is seen as wicked; but when he is the hero's enemy, she is regarded as helpful if not necessarily virtuous. Thus, to a certain extent, her virtue is a function of the status of her husband, who is sometimes described as an Asura (a demonic enemy and older brother of the gods) but sometimes as a Gandharva, a demigod of hazier moral status: he is the source of positive powers of fertility, but sometimes he sides with the Asuras against the gods. This mugwump quality of the Gandharva is clear from a brief episode in which no woman plays a part.

The Gandharva in the Middle (*JB* 1. 154–55)

The gods, fathers, and men were on one side, and the Asuras, Rakṣases [ogres], and Piśācas [ghouls] were on the other. They were contending for these three worlds. Now the Kalis, who were Gandharvas, were moving about in the middle, honoring neither one side of them nor the other. The gods, fathers, and men overcame the Asuras, Rakṣases, and Piśācas and divided the three worlds among them: the gods took as their share the world of the gods, the fathers took the world of the fathers, and the men took the world of men. Then the Kali Gandharvas came there and said, "Give us a share in these worlds, now that it is all over." "No," they answered, "you went back and forth without honoring one side or the other." "But we did honor you in our *minds*," the Gandharvas replied; "so give us a share, now that it is all over." "No," they replied; "we have divided these worlds up properly; we cannot mix it all together again." The Gandharvas said, "Let us have just what we see right here." So they gave them the Kalindas.

Since the Gandharvas are technically not demons, their assistance to the gods is a matter of strategic alliance, not a betrayal of their own side. Yet there is a minor overtone of betrayal, for the Gandharvas are often listed with the Asuras and Piśācas in catalogues of supernatural beings, and the lame assertion that they were "mentally" on the side of the gods (though this is supported by the Vedic tradition of "mentally" performing a sacrifice) is not entirely persuasive. The gods therefore give them merely the land of the Kalindas, a mountainous border area, associated in mythology with outcastes and sinners—liminal people, like the Gandharvas themselves.

The real traitor in this cycle, however, is not the Gandharva but his wife, who gives the gods information that her husband does not wish them to have.

The Wife of the Gandharva of the Waters (*JB* 1. 125–27)

The gods and demons were fighting, but there was no decisive victory. Bṛhaspati was the domestic priest of the gods, and Uśanas Kāvya was the priest of the demons [Asuras]. Whatever [the gods] did forwards in a ritual, [the demons] did backwards, and thus, since all was equaled out, the rite had no effect. A three-headed Gandharva knew which of them would win, for he moved about on a boat-city floating in the middle of the waters.

Indra knew that the three-headed Gandharva knew about the victory, and he charmed his [the Gandharva's] wife. Lusting for the victory, he said to her, "Ask your husband which of these will win, for the gods and demons are struggling without any decisive victory." The Gandharva came upon the two of them as they were conversing, and Indra hid himself on the side of the ship, taking the form of a leech or a blade of grass. Then she asked her husband, "Which of these will win? For the gods and demons are struggling without any decisive victory."

"Not so loud," he said, "the earth has ears." And so even now they say, "Not so loud, the earth has ears." "No," she said, "tell me." He said, "These two Brahmins are equal in their knowledge, Bṛhaspati among the gods, and Uśanas Kāvya among the demons. What the two do comes out the same; whatever oblation one makes, the other makes. These two [offerings] meet and return, neutralized. But if one of the two of them goes over to the other side, that side will win." As

soon as Indra learned this, he became a green parrot and flew up; and when [the Gandharva] looked after him as he flew up, he said, "Those for whom this green one flies, they will win."

[Indra] came to Kāvya Uśanas among the demons, and he said to him, "Great sage, which people are you helping to prosper? You are ours, and we are yours. Help us." "How?" he asked; "What will you tempt me with?" "With these wishing-cows of Virocana, the son of Prahlāda." So Indra won him over, and they ran forth; but the demons took after them and followed the two of them. Then Indra said, "Great sage, these demons are following the two of us." Then he [Kāvya Uśanas] said, "Do something so that they do not follow us." The two of them resorted to this verse [*RV* 9. 87. 2]: "The Soma drop with its good weapons purifies itself, protecting the sacrificer; father of gods, . . . engenderer, clever, he is the pillar of heaven, the support of the earth." With this they built a pillar up to heaven, and the demons could not go beyond it. Then the two of them went with the wishing-cows to the gods, and when they arrived they celebrated with this verse [*RV* 9. 87. 3]: "The inspired sage, Uśanas with his poetry, . . . discovered what had been hidden, the secret, concealed name of the cows." These are verses for cattle; whoever praises with these verses gets cattle. The chant of Uśanas is about them; for Uśanas Kāvya wished for the immortal world of the Gandharvas among the gods. He saw this chant and praised with it, and thereby he won the immortal Gandharva world among the gods.

Part of the complexity of of this tale arises from the fact that, with regard to the matter of Uśanas's natural allegiance, the text is at cross-purposes with the Vedic verses that it purports to gloss. In the verses, and in the closing lines of the *Jaiminīya* text, Uśanas is one of the ancient titans (Asuras), not yet defined as enemies of the gods, and he aspires to the highest world of the gods, the world of the Gandharva in the waters, who is a common Ṛg Vedic personification of the sun.

Uśanas helps Indra to win this world—to win the cows that are symbolic of Soma and immortality and the sun; in the *Ṛg Veda*, he accomplishes this by finding the cows in the cave (*RV* 3. 31; O'Flaherty 1981, pp. 151–55). The text of the Brāhmaṇa, by contrast, reduces both Uśanas and the Gandharvas to lower classes of beings: Uśanas becomes a treacherous Asura (now defined as a demonic enemy), and the Gandharva in the waters is no longer the sun but merely an unnamed Gandharva who happens to live on a boat in the water. Characteristically, the *Jaiminīya* has acted out a cosmic metaphor on the reduced, intimate, human level.

In the *Jaiminīya* text, the gods bribe Uśanas with wish-granting verses that are also wish-granting cows. The only other text that tells this story at any length is one that is closely related to the *Jaiminīya*: the *Baudhāyana Śrauta Sūtra*. This text tells the tale in less detail than the *Jaiminīya* and omits the final episode of the cows; instead, the wish-granting cows (no longer connected with Vedic verses) are associated with a woman, and the central woman in the story is more explicitly erotic in her relationship with Indra:

As the gods and demons were fighting, they divided all that they possessed into two parts: the gods took some, and the demons took some. Bṛhaspati was the domestic priest [Purohita] of the gods, and Uśanas Kāvya [was the priest] of the demons; both the gods and the demons had their own Brahmin. They fought countless battles, in which neither side won the decisive victory. No one in the two armies knew what the outcome would be, but the Gandharva Sūryavarcas ["Glory of the Sun"] knew. Indra was on joking terms with the Gandharva's wife. He said to her, "My lovely one, ask the Gandharva why there is no decisive outcome between the gods and the demons." "Fine," she said, "come back yourself in the morning."

Now the Gandharva had made a golden palace floating in the middle of the sea. Indra turned himself into a golden sunbeam and came there and lay down close to the ship's

cabin. When the Gandharva's wife noticed that Indra had come, she said [to her husband], "My handsome one, tell me why there can be no decisive victory between gods and demons." "Not so loud," he replied, "the ship has ears. Both the gods and the demons have a Brahmin." As he heard these words, Indra the Golden One took the form of a green parrot and flew up. The Gandharva saw him and said, "O mighty lord, whatever side the Golden One is on, they will win."

Indra went away from there and went to Uśanas, to win him over, promising him that he would receive his [Indra's] daughter Jayantī and four wishing-cows. This won Uśanas over, and he abandoned the demons and went over to the gods. [*BŚS* 18. 46]

The "joking relationship" that Indra has with the Gandharva's wife is the usual Vedic euphemism for an affair with a married woman (cf. *BAU* 6. 4. 12). This text is in this respect slightly more explicit than the *Jaiminīya*, but all else in the *Baudhāyana* version is condensed in comparison with the *Jaiminīya*.

Another contemporary version of the theme is similarly colorless when set beside our proof text, though it provides an ironic twist by replacing the Gandharva's wife with the wife of Indra himself:

The gods asked Indra to give them a share in the sacrifice, but he just looked at them. Then the gods said, "Here is the dear wife, the favorite wife, of Indra, named Prāsahā; let us seek what we want from her." "Fine," they agreed. They sought what they wanted from her, and she said to them, "I will tell you in the morning." Therefore wives seek what they want from a husband, and therefore a wife seeks what she wants from her husband in the night. They went to her in the morning, and she replied with this verse [*RV* 10. 74. 6]: "When the shatterer of citadels won the highest place, he made good his name, Killer of Vṛtra. He revealed himself as the powerful Husband of Force [*prāsah*]." The powerful

Husband of Force is Indra. "Let him do what we want him to do" [they said to Prāsahā]. And indeed she said to them, "He has done what we have said." Then the gods said, "Let her also have a share, since she has not yet got a share in what is ours." "Fine," they said, and they gave her a share. [*AB* 3. 21–22]

Though this text does not tell us precisely what wiles she used, Prāsahā manages in the night to get Indra to do what the gods have asked. In return, she is given not wishing-cows or hymns but simply a share in the sacrifice—a share of the share that she wheedles out of her husband for the other gods. Such are the uses of pillow-talk, in this world as in heaven.

The treachery of the wife has nothing to do with the treachery of the husband; the wife betrays her husband whether he is a god (like Indra) or a Gandharva (like Sūryavarcas) or a demon (like Uśanas). The last category is by far the most prevalent in the mythology of the Brāhmaṇas, but there is a tale in the *Jaiminīya* that assimilates the problems of a married human man to this genre. The cuckolder, though not, this time, the cuckold, is a Gandharva.

The Mortal's Wife and the Dangerous Sacrifice (*JB* 2. 126)

Udara, the son of Śaṇḍila, wished to perform the Ekatrika sacrifice, and he made his decision in his mind, but he did not tell anyone about it. His wife was possessed by a Gandharva [*Gandharviṇī*]. This Gandharva approached her and said, "There is a rather dangerous sacrifice called the Ekatrika, and your husband wants to perform it." She said to her husband, "The Ekatrika sacrifice is rather dangerous. Do you really want to perform that sacrifice?" He said to her, "I never mentioned this to anyone; it was just a decision in my own mind. Who told you about it?" "A certain Gandharva approached me." "Then you must ask him: Will he or will he not accomplish the sacrifice?" She asked [the Gandharva],

"Will he or will he not accomplish the sacrifice?" He replied, "We know it just as he knows it, but he knows it in one way, and I know it in another. And only the one who knows it my way will be able to accomplish the sacrifice." [Udara] did not dare to accomplish that sacrifice. But still Udara, the son of Śaṇḍila, became praiseworthy when in his mind alone he wished to perform the Ekatrika sacrifice. For this sacrifice has a double nature: whoever performs it either becomes very praiseworthy, or he becomes very evil.

The "mental sacrifice" that the Kali Gandharvas said they had performed is here performed by a man in conflict with a Gandharva. In its dynamics the tale resembles the story of Cyavana and the Aśvins (as well as the story of Indra and Upamā): the mortal man's wife is coveted by a supernatural being. Cyavana's wife remains steadfast and betrays her would-be seducers to her husband; the virtue of Udara Śaṇḍila's wife (like that of Upamā) remains somewhat in doubt, but it appears that she reveals the Gandharva's warning to her husband at least in part out of wifely concern for his safety, as well as out of simple, indiscreet garrulousness. And just as Cyavana then enlists his wife's aid to use the seducers (the Aśvins) to accomplish what he wants, so, too, Udara persuades his wife to question the Gandharva on his behalf. Udara does not gain so dramatic a boon as Cyavana did, for the Gandharva is not as powerful as the Aśvins; Udara does not even learn how to perform the dangerous Ekatrika sacrifice (which some other mortals did perform successfully), but at any rate he learns *not* to perform it and to settle for the benefits of having performed it mentally.

Thus the woman can be said to have betrayed the Gandharva to her husband by repeating to him the advice that, one may assume (from the pattern of the stories of "pillow-talk" that we have already seen), the Gandharva did not intend him to have. Has she also betrayed her husband with (or to) the Gandharva? It is hard to be certain of this. The Gandharva in this text is said to have possessed her; this may well be a reference to the Ṛg Vedic belief that the Gandharva had the *droit de seigneur* to every bride; it was he who took her maidenhead and absorbed some of the dangerous magic connected with defloration (*RV* 10. 85; O'Flaherty 1981, pp. 267–74). In this way the Gandharva, at the time of the wedding, performs an ambiguous service for the husband, cuckolding him (represented in the part of the Vedic hymn that begs the Gandharva to give the bride back to her husband) but also standing in for him at a dangerous moment. This same ambiguity is evident in the story of Udara. The woman, in her turn, may be said to "re-rat" (to use Churchill's vivid term), a characteristic trait of women in Indian folklore: they betray *everyone*, but they can also be helpful to everyone; it depends on whether one regards the glass as half full or half empty. So, too, the Gandharvas, who are associated with fertility but also with eroticism, are active both as seducers and as seduced, mediating between these two groups even as they mediate between gods and demons. Indeed, the several sets of pairs (seducer/seduced, gods/demons, Gandharvas/women) intertwine throughout the *Jaiminīya*, for the Gandharvas help the gods to seduce and destroy demonic women who have tried to betray and seduce demons, men, and even gods.

The same Aśvins who test and assist Cyavana help another sage in the following story.

The Lover of the Demon's Daughter (*JB* 3. 72–74)

Kaṇva Nārṣada married the daughter of the demon Akhaga ["Non-Sky-going"] and begat two sons on her, Triśoka ["Triple Sorrow"] and Nabhāka ["Little Sky"]. She got angry with him and went back to her relatives, but he went after her. The demons smeared a blinding ointment on him [on the eyes] and said to him, "If you are a true Brahmin, tell us when it is daybreak." The two Aśvins found out about all this, for the Aśvins are the ones among the gods who set free people who are imprisoned. They went up to him, unseen, and said, "When we pass by directly above you and sound the

lute, then tell them that it is daybreak." During the night the demons kept jumping up and saying, "Get up, wake up, yoke your ploughs, it's daybreak." But he would say, "No, it is *not* daybreak." Then the two Aśvins passed by right over him and sounded the lute, and he said, "Take this away, for now it is daybreak; yoke your ploughs."

Then they said, "This seer [*ṛṣi*] really is a Brahmin. It's a bad thing to take away *his* wife. Hell, let's give her back to him." They gave her back to him, and she said to him, "They want to kill you, but in a sneaky, secret way. I have heard them plotting. They will put a golden seat in the shade for you, but do not sit on it." The demons came forward and put a golden seat down for him; but foolishly he sat down on it, and it turned to stone and held him fast. Then Triśoka and Nabhāka, his sons, found out that the demons had entrapped their father in stone. They came to him, and Nabhāka wished, "Let me deceive them." He saw the Nabhāka chant and sang it over [the chair], and he [Kaṇva] became visible in it the way the string of a necklace is visible inside the jewels. Then Triśoka wished, "Let me throw [the chair] apart." He saw the Traiśoka chant and with it made [the chair] fall into two pieces. Kaṇva was still unconscious, but he came out of [the chair]. He [Triśoka] wished, "Let him live," and touched him, saying "Hey! Live!" He came to life, but there was darkness [i.e., blindness] over him. Then [Triśoka] wished, "Let it be day for him," and he touched him, saying, "Hey! Day!" And there was daylight for him. Then he wished, "Let me make him reach the world of heaven," and he touched him and said, "Hey! Heaven!" And he made him go to the world of heaven.

This is a story of brothers as well as a story of fathers and sons, but it is also a story about a dangerous woman who marries a sage and bears him sons, then leaves him, but finally returns in time to save his life (betraying her own people, the demons).

The story of the daughter of a demon who betrays her people in order to save her nondemonic lover is an ancient

Indo-European theme that is widespread in India; it appears in the *Mahābhārata* as the tale of Kaca and Devayānī (*MBh* 1. 71; O'Flaherty 1975, pp. 281–89). The *Jaiminīya* tells other variants of this same general theme. One of them is this story:

The Girl on the Island (*JB* 3. 197)

The Śāktyas, who offer meat cakes, were having a sacrifice. Gaurivīti, a son of Śakti, killed a deer. [The eagle named] Tārkṣya Suparṇa came flying to him from above. Gaurivīti aimed at Suparṇa, and the bird said, "Sage, do not shoot at me. Whatever you desire, I will fulfill it for you." "What desire do I have?" asked Gaurivīti. "You desire the daughter of Asita Dhāmnya. I will take you to her." Now, Asita Dhāmnya was jealous. His palace was in the middle realm of air, and there they guarded his daughter. The bird concealed Gaurivīti in the stalk of a leaf and carried him to the girl. Then, by means of the special chant, "Lover, awaken," he awakened him at dawn. That is why the "Lover, awaken," chant has that name.

The girl became pregnant and bore a son. The demons tore him apart and threw him away, saying, "This is the child of a sister [*jāmīgarbha,* i.e., born of a man and his twin sister, too closely related]; some ogre [Rākṣasa] begat it." He [Gaurivīti] wished, "Let me revive him." He saw this chant and revived him with it, and the child became Saṃkṛti, the son of Gaurivīti.

That the woman in this story is a demon is not explicit until her child is born and rejected by the demons, for a reason that remains obscure; perhaps "child of incest" is a general term of opprobrium, or perhaps the demons argue that since the girl was guarded only by her close kin—or by a lower type of demon, an ogre—one of them must have been the father. In any case, they regard the child as illegitimate. The demons try to destroy not the father (as in the tale of Kaṇva) but the son (as in the more widespread tale of the birth of the hero to supernatural parents, of which we have seen a variant in the story of "The Uncle Who Tried to Murder the Newborn Child").

Though the woman in the tale of Gaurivīti is ambivalent in her relationship to him (she gets him out of the trouble he would not have had had he not fallen in love with her), she is, when all is said and done, loyal to him; she is his wife (by common law—the Gandharva rite, as it is called in India), and she procures for him the mandatory happy ending. The full force of the fear of women is never revealed in the stories of demidemonic wives; it is deflected onto the stories of unmarried full demonesses, to which we will now turn.

6
The Fear of Demonic Women

Women and demons are dangerous; demonic women are *very* dangerous. Thus, even though, in the *Jaiminīya*, all dangers are always overcome, the hero who encounters certain *femmes fatales* is often in fear of his life—until the very last moment, when all comes right again.

We have seen the moral ambivalence of the women associated with the Gandharvas (themselves liminal), but even the women associated with the more obviously villainous Asuras (demons) are complex in their relationship to evil in the *Jaiminīya*. Such a woman is Saramā, the bitch of the gods. Her story is first told in a fairly straightforward dialogue in the *Ṛg Veda*, in which demons named Paṇis have stolen the cows belonging to the gods and sages and have hidden them in a mountain cave. Indra and the gods send Saramā to follow the trail of the cows; this leads her to the Paṇis, who try in vain to persuade her to betray the gods. The hymn ends as she warns the Paṇis that Indra and the gods will come and take the cows away (*RV* 10. 108; O'Flaherty 1981, pp. 156–57; O'Flaherty 1975, pp. 73–74). The *Jaiminīya* not only expands this episode but adds an entirely new prelude to it.

The Divine Bitch (*JB* 2. 440–42)

The Asuras named Paṇis were the cowherds of the gods. They went off with [the cows] and penned them up in the

Rasā [river] and hid them in a cave. The gods complained, "Suparṇa ["Fine-feathered," the name of an eagle], search for these cows of ours." "All right," he said, and flew after them; and he came upon them hidden in a cave beside the Rasā. As he arrived, they placed before him melted butter, milk, curds, and whey, which were very pleasing to him, and they said to him, "Suparṇa, this food will be an offering for you. Do not betray us." He flew away again, and the gods said to him, "Suparṇa, have you found our cows?" But when he said, "What news is there about the cows?", Indra squeezed his throat and said to him, "*This* is the news about the cows. Your mouth [tells that] you stayed among the cows." The bird then vomited a drop of sour milk or curds, which became the camphor plant that grows in the spring. Then Indra cursed him, saying, "Unclean and vile will be your livelihood, since you found our cows and did not tell us." And so his livelihood is the most evil stuff that is in the back half of the village.

The gods then said to Saramā, "Saramā, search for those cows of ours." "All right," she said, and went after them. When she came to the Rasā, which flows deep on this side of the ocean, she said to her [the river], "I will swim you; you should let me ford you." "Swim me," replied the river, "but I will not let you ford me." Saramā laid back her ears and rushed forward, about to swim, but the river reflected, "How should a bitch swim me? Hell, I will let her ford me." And she said to her, "Do not swim me; I will let you ford me." "All right," she said, and she crossed over by the ford that was made for her. Then she came upon the cows, hidden within a cave beside the Rasā, and, as she arrived, they placed before her in the same way [as they had for the eagle] melted butter, milk, curds, and whey. But she said, "I am not so unfriendly to the gods; I have found the cows that I want to get from you. You stole them from the gods, but I am the one who followed the track made by the cows. You will not talk me out of it, nor will you keep Indra's cows." She remained there, but she did

not eat; she found the outer membrane of the waters, and she ate that. Then someone sang out about her, "Saramā is eating the outer membrane as if she were killing someone." And even now there is this reproach, "Saramā is eating the outer membrane as if she were killing someone," for she did eat the membrane. Then she went back again, and they said to her, "Saramā, have you found the cows?" "I found them," she said, "hidden in a cave beside the Rasā. Take them just as you wanted to." Indra said to her, "Since you found our cows, I make your progeny eaters of food." And indeed, among the Vidarbhas the brindled dogs descended from Saramā [*sārameyas*] kill even tigers.

The new prelude is a pastiche of several Vedic motifs: the eagle who flies with Indra to fetch back the Soma (which has been taken by the demons, or which simply sprouts in heaven [*RV* 4. 26–27; O'Flaherty 1981, pp. 128–30]); the cows penned up in a cave by the Paṇis (*RV* 3. 31; O'Flaherty 1981, pp. 151–55); and the betrayal of the demons by Agni and Soma (*RV* 10. 124; O'Flaherty 1981, pp. 110–11). The particular element that the *Jaiminīya* introduces in order to fuse these tales, to one another and to the story of Saramā, is the theme of the unclean food of the demons, the forbidden food that poisons you. (This motif is one to which the *Jaiminīya* devotes much attention; cf. *JB* 1. 223; 2. 83–84; 3. 139; 3. 251.)

This theme of unclean food is then highlighted when the *Jaiminīya* goes on to tell its own version of the tale of Saramā. For whereas in the *Ṛg Veda* the Paṇis attempted to bribe Saramā merely with vague promises of "sisterhood" with them and "a share of the cattle" (the usual Vedic bribe), in the *Jaiminīya* they offer her specific foods, which she rejects. She does, however, eat the outer membrane of the waters, and in this she is doing a good thing: she is releasing the cows so that they can be born out of the cave that is their imprisoning womb. But this action is also censured as a kind of pseudo-murder (perhaps a crude form of abortion). Saramā is thus both good—she resists the temptation to eat the food of the demons, and she destroys the imprisoning membrane—and evil—she does eat the outer membrane. The *Jaiminīya* has taken the motif of treachery and made it dialectic, recasting it in the context of the tale of the Soma-bringing eagle and the carrion-eating vulture, the witch who eats embryos and the bitch who eats the unclean amniotic sac.

Saramā persists in Vedic literature as the long-tongued dog who defiles the sacrifice. The *Ṛg Veda* warns the sacrificer to "Pierce the long-tongued dog away" (*RV* 9. 101. 1), and this image is ultimately developed into an episode in the *Mahābhārata,* in which Saramā herself curses several kings because they had kicked one of her sons out of their sacrificial grounds when he had not even looked at the oblations, let alone licked them (*MBh* 1. 3. 1–10). Between the *Ṛg Veda* and the *Mahābhārata*, as is so often the case, the *Jaiminīya* supplies the essential link. Other Epic passages speak of the defiling tongue of a male dog in a sexual context: a sage setting out on a journey asks his pupil to protect his (the sage's) wife "so that the Indra of the gods will not lap her up as a wicked dog laps up the sacrificial oblation" (*MBh* 13. 40. 39); and when Rāma rejects Sītā after she has lived in the palace of the demon Rāvaṇa, he compares her to an oblation that has been licked by a dog (*MBh* 3. 275. 14). So, too, several Brāhmaṇas speak of a demonic female named Long-Tongue—not a dog—who licks the milk offering and curdles it (*KāṭhB* 29. 1; *MS* 3. 10. 6; *AB* 2. 22. 10). Other Brāhmaṇas also contain brief references to an ogress (Rākṣasī) named Long-Tongue, whom Indra had Sumitra, the son of Kutsa, seduce and kill (*PB* 13. 6. 9–10; see also Sāyaṇa on *RV* 1. 97), and to another demoness (unnamed), who had vaginas on every limb, and whom Indra destroyed (at his own peril) by seducing her, placing penises on each of his joints (*KB* 23. 4). Whether all of these texts are refracting small pieces of a story that they knew from the *Jaiminīya* or whether the *Jaiminīya* put together the full story from all of these disparate scraps, is difficult to judge. But the story is told in full only in the *Jaiminīya*, and it is quite a story.

LONG-TONGUE THE DEMONESS (*JB* 1. 161–63)

"Long-Tongue" [Dīrghajihvī] was a demoness, and she used to lick at the Soma and lick at the Soma all the time. She lived in the northern ocean (or Soma pot), and she licked up the Soma that was pressed in the southern, eastern, and western oceans. Indra wanted to grab her, but he could not get hold of her. So he said, "Let no one perform any sacrifices at all, for Long-Tongue licks up the Soma and licks up the Soma." Now, Sumitra, the son of Kutsa, was handsome. Indra said to him, "Sumitra, you are good-looking. Women like to flirt with a good-looking man. Flirt with this Long-Tongue." Sumitra went to her and said, "Long-Tongue, make love with me." She said, "You have just one penis, but I have mice [i.e., vaginas] on every limb, on this limb and that limb. This won't work." He went back and said to Indra, "She said to me, 'You have just one penis, but I have mice on every limb, on this limb and that limb. This won't work.'" "I will make penises for you on every limb," said Indra. Equipped with these, Sumitra went back to her and said to her, "Long-Tongue, make love with me." When she repeated her earlier complaint, he said, "I have penises on every limb." "Aha! Let me see your body," she said.

He showed them to her, and they made her very happy. "Come," she said, "what's your name?" "Sumitra [Good Friend]." "That's a lovely name." They lay together. As soon as he had his way with her, he remained firmly stuck in her. Then she said, "Sir, didn't you say you were a Good Friend?" He replied, "I am indeed a good friend to a good friend, but I am a bad friend to a bad friend." He saw these Sumitra chants and praised with them, and with them he summoned Indra.

Indra ran against her and struck her down with his thun-

derbolt, which was this verse: "To keep the pressed drink at its best and most intoxicating, my friends, pierce away the long-tongued dog" [*RV* 9. 101.1]. And with that verse he killed her. These are the verses that slay fraternal rivals and that slay ogres [Rakṣases]. Whoever praises with these chants slays his hateful fraternal rivals and drives away all evil demons.

This story hardly requires a lengthy scholarly commentary, but there are some interesting links with other *Jaiminīya* cycles and other Vedic texts. Kutsa, here the father of the boy to whom Indra gives extra penises, appears elsewhere as the one who attacks Indra's testicles. Like the wife of Triyaruṇa, Long-Tongue has unusual sexual powers, which are at once her weapon and her vulnerability: hoist by her own petard, as it were, she is immobilized by being sexually pinned down in a thousand places (an image perhaps suggested by observations of mating dogs, similarly paralyzed). The leap from the Ṛg Vedic verse of the dog licking the oblation to the grotesque sexual deformities described in the *Jaiminīya* is considerable; it may be a clue to the kind of pressure building up in the *Jaiminīya*, a pressure not necessarily of personal obsessions but rather a backlog of folktales (themselves perhaps built out of personal obsessions). These tales burst out when the name "Long-Tongue" unleashes a flood of nightmare images—images of sexual danger. For the excessive genitals of the demoness make her sexually dangerous, even as her excessively long tongue (which may also have phallic implications) makes her ritually dangerous. This long tongue later becomes an attribute of the bloodthirsty and sexually voracious goddess Kālī (O'Flaherty 1980a, p. 85).

Saramā and Long-Tongue are females who poison the sacrificial food. Saramā is literally a bitch, while Long-Tongue is a demoness with certain bitch-like traits. The cycle of stories in which Indra becomes sexually involved with such bestial and/or demonic women reveals a consistent pattern. Indra is a powerful father in strong competition—often sexual competition—with his sons and with worshipers. Although occasionally (as in "Kutsa Seduces Indra's Wife" [*JB* 3. 199–200]) one encounters an episode that includes the third member of the triangle—the mother—her role was usually displaced onto symbolic mothers: female animals and ogresses. But so thoroughly ingrained is the *Jaiminīya*'s habit of deflecting incestuous encounters into the nonhuman world that any attempt to decode them mechanically, to read these encounters in anthropomorphic terms, results in distortions and confusions. The ogresses of the *Jaiminīya* cannot simply be turned back into mothers and/or wives, though they do express the shadow side of women.

Of all the females in the *Jaiminīya*, Long-Tongue is the most bestial, the most grotesque, and the most dangerous; yet even she ultimately does no harm and is herself destroyed. She is more sinned against than sinning. The woman is the symbol of danger, but the point of the Brāhmaṇa is that danger is not, ultimately, dangerous—for the man who knows the chants.

Indeed, sometimes the chant that the man knows is expressly said to be a chant that gives him power over women. We have already seen how useful such power can be when the sacrificer uses his wife to obtain special knowledge. But the power over women can also boomerang when it is used not for sacrificial purposes but simply for erotic ends. In one such story, a man's desire to make all women desire him is his undoing.

How Not to Get to Heaven (*JB* 3. 270–71)

The sages said, "Come, let us conquer the world of heaven that is beyond the eagle, where those Atharvans dwell." Preṇin, the son of Somāhita, Madhucchandas, the son of Viśvāmitra, Asita, the son of Devala, and others wished to see the Atharvans; but although they performed their sacrifices for many years, the Atharvans did not notice them. At last the Atharvans noticed them and realized, "They are

doing the *śarauṣat* and the *vaṣat* [words chanted in the ritual], and so forth." Then Udvanta, one of the Atharvans, went down to them with a [Soma] bowl in his hand, and he said to them, "With what desires are you sacrificing?" "We wish to win the world of heaven that is beyond the eagle, where you Atharvans dwell."

He said to them, "Do you go behind the village?" "Yes." "What for?" "To the road." "Ah," he said, "that is not the way for you to get to heaven." And he looked into his Soma bowl. Then he said, "Do you eat meat?" "Yes." "What for?" "For eyesight and breath." "Ah," he said, "that is not the way for you to get to heaven." And he looked into his bowl. Then he said, "Do you go to women?" "Yes." "What for?" "To carry on the family line and not to be cut off." "Ah," he said, "that won't get you to heaven." And he looked down into his bowl. Then he said, "Do you tell lies?" "Yes." "What for?" "Because we lust for women, or for amusement, or in order to make friends." "Ah," said he, "get up and tell me your wishes, but you haven't got a hope of conquering the world of heaven."

Now Preṇin, the son of Somāhita, was a sinner. He said, "I will take the bad seed of seven rams, and whatever woman I say 'Hey!' to, let that woman desire me." And Madhucchandas, the son of Viśvāmitra, said, "I choose to have the mouth of a Brahmin." But Asita, the son of Devala, said, "Let me look down into that Soma bowl." Udvanta said, "Of all of these, he alone made a real choice." Asita looked down into the bowl and saw this chant and praised with it: "For riches, O Agni, we would kindle you; we pray to you for a powerful oblation on heaven and earth, O bull" [*SV* 1. 93a]. Now heaven and earth are all these worlds, and thus he moved along all these worlds. In the morning he stayed at the meeting of the gods, at noon at the meeting of men, and in the afternoon at the meeting of the fathers . . . .

Instead of using women to master the power of the sacrifice,

Preṇin passes up a chance to win all the worlds of the sacrifice when he chooses, instead, to become irresistible to women.

In another tale, this same talent, in the hands of a Brahmin named Yavakrī, leads not merely to the loss of heaven but to a gory and appropriately erotic end. The ambivalence of the danger posed by the sexual woman is the central theme of this complex tale, in which there are two women, a virtuous queen and a demonic woman who impersonates her, as well as two sexually dangerous men: a lascivious priest and a hideous Gandharva, whom he inadvertently cuckolds. This final story thoroughly mixes the species (human and demonic) and sets the encounter in the frame of a parallel conflict that is central to the *Jaiminīya*, the conflict between kings and priests.

The Brahmin's Wife with Hair on the Soles of Her Feet (*JB* 2. 269–72)

Mauṇḍibha Udanyu, the king of the Udanyus, performed a horse sacrifice. Yavakrī, the son of Somastamba, sat there in a challenging position. The priests of Mauṇḍibha took as the opening verses of the sacrifice the phrase "This Pūṣan, wealth, good fortune" [*SV* 2. 168–70]. Then Yavakrī said, "Because you have made a mistake [in choosing these verses], Mauṇḍibha, in a month you will lose your life." This was his curse. Now, Mauṇḍibha Udanyu had the triple knowledge [of past, present, and future], and he said, "Scatter my sacrificial implements, and smear my houses with mud, as a pledge: When this Brahmin with his curse dies, then I will sacrifice." They smeared his houses with mud and took this as a pledge.

Now, Yavakrī had the glory and glamor of a Brahmin; if he called a woman to him and said "Hey!" to her, she made love with him and she died; and even if she did not make love with him, she died. He called the wife of Yajñavacas, the son of Rājastamba, to him and said "Hey!" to her. She reflected, "If I make love with him, or if I do not, I will surely die in any

case. Hell, let me make love with him; if I am to die, let me at least die giving pleasure to a Brahmin." She said to him, "Stay there, and I will come to you."

As she was preparing herself, weeping, her husband came to her. He said to her, "Why are you adorning yourself, and why are you weeping?" She said, "I am full of self-pity when I realize that I am going to die. For Yavakrī called me to him and said 'Hey!' to me. " He [her husband] said, "Bring me some sacrificial butter." After he had purified the butter with the two strainers, he made an oblation and said, "Agni, bring to me Preṇī, beloved of Agni, prepared and adorned for Bharadvāja's descendant [Yavakrī], and she will save me today. Svāhā! [Amen!]." And with this he created a nymph [Apsaras] of the same form [as his wife], and he said to her, "There is Yavakrī. Go to him." Then he made a second oblation and said, "Bring me a fierce Gandharva, lusty, rock-hurling, blindingly bright, to be the killer of Bharadvāja's descendant. Svāhā!" And with this he created a jealous Gandharva with an iron club in his hand, and he said to him, "Your wife has just gone to Yavakrī. Go to him."

As [the nymph] came to [Yavakrī], Yavakrī spread out the bed, and she smiled at him. He said to her, "Little woman, you're smiling, but you don't have anything to smile about." "Why so?" "Because you are going to die," he said. She stretched out her foot and said, "Man, you have surely never 'cooked' a woman with feet like this." For the bottoms of her feet were covered with hair. The two of them went together, and when they finally pulled apart, just at that moment the Gandharva with the iron club in his hand came to them. Yavakrī said to him, "Honor to you. How can I avoid paying for this?" "Maybe there is a way for you to make up for it, and maybe there is not," said [the Gandharva]. "If you cut off the head of everything that your father possesses, before sunrise, that might make up for it—or maybe it won't."

Yavakrī began to cut [off the heads] in that way. People said, "Yavakrī has gone crazy. Let's tie him up." "No," said

his father; "my son acts as if he is driven by the gods. He is the one who knows what is best to do in this matter." Now, there was a woodcutter in the village who was deaf, and so he had not heard the prohibition [against stopping Yavakrī]. Yavakrī came to him and began cutting off his [animals' heads]. The woodcutter said, "What person is this [who is] ruining us?"; and he killed Yavakrī—this is what some people say. But others say that the sun rose and shone upon Yavakrī as he was still slaughtering the cattle, and, as the sun rose, the Gandharva killed him. In any case, he died; that is what did happen. But doubtless it was the Gandharva who killed him [directly or indirectly].

Now when Mauṇḍibha found out about this, he said, "Rebuild the sacrificial implements and perform the sacrifice for me, Brahmins. The Brahmin who cursed me has died." They performed the sacrifice for him, and, when Somastamba found out about it, he came there and sat down in the same way [as his son Yavakrī had done]. And Somastamba said, "This so-called nobleman in name only [i.e., King Mauṇḍibha] does not understand the sacrifice that he has had performed. Nor did he kill my son with his words. That was simply the exact duration of my son's life-span." And he cursed him for that, saying, "This nobleman in name only will die, and the descendants of Mauṇḍibha will be servants." These are the Gotamas, who are said to be servants.

Most of this story is abundantly clear, both in its own right and in the context of other *Jaiminīya* stories, but there are a few points in need of clarification. Mauṇḍibha is a king, but Yavakrī and Yajñavacas (the husband of the woman whom Yavakrī seduces) are Brahmins; this is a tale of Brahmin versus Brahmin, not just Brahmin versus king. This point is made clear when Yavakrī's father appears on the scene at the end and assures Mauṇḍibha that he (the king) could not have killed Yavakrī, who was undone by his own deeds (his own preordained life-span, the fulfillment of his own karma)—and, he might have added, by one of his own kind, another priest. The king's pledge (to destroy his own property as a kind of implicit vow that Yavakrī would die) has an effect on his own life (it eventually enables him to perform a sacrifice that will not fail) but not on Yavakrī's.

Yavakrī is destroyed by his own rampant sexuality. The charm that he uses (saying "Hey!" to any woman he wants) is the same charm that is used by the sinful Preṇin (*JB* 3. 270–71), who appears in the Yavakrī story in a modified form: he has become a female, the Preṇī who is the nymph who gets Yavakrī. But Yavakrī does not just lure women with his magic powers (as Preṇin does); he kills them (as Sumitra does), whether he makes love to them or not. This sadism, which also drives him to taunt the woman with her imminent death when she smiles at him, is closely linked to the sexual voracity that is his nemesis. The woman whom he mistakes for the wife of Yajñavacas uses obscene language, which no Brahmin's wife would use (the phrase that I have translated as "cooked a woman" [cf. the American "get hot for a woman"], which Caland drily suggests may be "slang for coitus"); she also has hair growing on the bottom of her feet, as no human woman would have. Nevertheless, he takes her to bed.

She, of course, "cooks" him, and her use of the metaphor of food to describe sexual intercourse links her to the genre of demonic women who devour the men they sleep with. Yet the text displaces the guilt from her to her true mate, the Gandharva with the club (reminiscent of the man with the club in "Bhṛgu's Journey in the Other World" [*JB* 1. 42–44] and the club of the wicked "Uncle Who Tried to Murder the Newborn Child" [*JB* 3. 221]). The danger posed by the human woman is further displaced by the creation of a demonic double, who goes to Yavakrī in her stead; for though the text warns against the dangers that come to the man who seduces the wife of a Brahmin (even when that Brahmin is "The Lover of the Demon's Daughter," [*JB* 3. 72–74]), it here distinguishes between virtuous mortal women and destructive demonic women, splitting away the good woman from her evil alter ego.

Yet another displacement may be seen if we view the tale of Yavakrī in the context of Brāhmaṇa mythology as a whole and in the context of the *Jaiminīya* corpus in particular: though Yavakrī's father does nothing to harm him, he also does nothing to help him when other men (the king and the other Brahmin) retaliate against Yavakrī's uncontrolled violence and lust. The father will not stop his son ("He knows what he is doing," he protests lamely when the villagers quite sensibly want to lock Yavakrī up to prevent the wholesale slaughter of their livestock); he lets others do it for him. It is not necessary, however, to draw this tale into the cycle of father-son conflicts; primarily, and quite clearly, it is a tale of male-female conflict, to which other themes have been assimilated and made subservient.

The villain of the piece is sexuality in any form, female or male: Yavakrī is his own seducer and his own destroyer. Yet there is much humor and affectionate observation of the creatures caught up in the web of their own lust, and there is much cynicism and satire in the depictions of those who think that they are above lust. Many of these qualities are retained in the retelling of the tale in the *Mahābhārata*, where, for once, it is told more briefly than in the *Jaiminīya*:

> **As the fearless Yavakrī was wandering about, he came in the springtime to the hermitage of Raibhya, a holy place adorned with flowering trees. There he saw the sage's daughter-in-law moving about like a nymph [Kiṃnarī]. Yavakrī's mind was stolen by lust, and he lost all sense of shame; he said to the shy woman, "Come to bed with me!" She knew his nature, and she was afraid he would curse her; so, although she was also aware of Raibhya's powers, she said, "Very well," and went with him. He brought her to a lonely spot and overwhelmed her. Then Raibhya returned to his hermitage, and when he saw that his daughter-in-law, the wife of Parāvasu, was weeping and in pain, he comforted her with gentle words and**

asked her what had happened. The good woman told him all that Yavakrī had said and what she had said to him in reply, after considering what was best.

When Raibhya heard what Yavakrī had done, his mind seemed to be on fire, and he was full of anger, overcome with fury. The hot-tempered ascetic tore out a handful of hair from his head and offered it as an oblation into the ritual fire. Then a woman came out of the fire, who matched the other woman in beauty. Once more he tore out a handful of hair and offered it into the fire, and from it there arose a gruesome ogre with horrible eyes. They said to Raibhya, "What should we do?" and the angry sage said, "Kill Yavakrī!" "Very well," they said, and went to hurt Yavakrī.

The witch who had been created by the noble sage went up to Yavakrī; she stole his water pot and seduced him. When Yavakrī had become unclean and had no water pot, the ogre raised a trident in his hand and rushed at him. When Yavakrī saw him rushing at him with a trident in his hand to hurt him, he quickly got up and ran to a pond. When he saw that the pond had no water left in it, he quickly went on to all the rivers, but they were all dried up too. As he was being chased by the hideous ogre with the trident in his hand, Yavakrī ran in terror to his father's sacrificial ground. But guarding the door was a blind servant, who held him back by force as he tried to enter and kept him there at the door. As Yavakrī was held there by the servant, the ogre beat him with the trident; and his heart split and he fell dead. When the ogre had killed Yavakrī, he went back to Raibhya, who dismissed him; and so off he went with the woman. [*MBh* 3. 137. 1–20]

This is a more human, less magical, text. Yavakrī in the Epic has no magical powers other than the same power to curse that all sages have; he succeeds in seducing the woman and is beaten to death, undone by a blind servant instead of a deaf woodcutter. The man who avenges the rape is the woman's father-in-law, not her husband, and Yavakrī's father never appears at all. There is poignancy in the Epic version of the story and some humor (in the sage's farcical attempts to rid himself of the pollution of sex). More important, the Epic has what the *Jaiminīya* can never have: tragedy. The woman really *is* raped, and Yavakrī's death cannot undo her shame. Ironically, the only one who experiences the happy ending in the Epic version of the story is the Gandharva; his fate is never spelled out in the *Jaiminīya* (though presumably he vanished when he had finished his work), but in the Epic he gets the girl. Despite the more serious human implications of the Epic narrative, however, it has lost the sinister conversations, the macabre details, and the magic transformations that give the *Jaiminīya* version its nightmare atmosphere.

But if these are nightmares, they are nightmares from which the dreamer knows he will awake; the terrible things that actually do happen in the Epic *almost* happen to the heroes in the *Jaiminīya*, but then, at the last minute, Victoria's messenger comes riding, the Marines land, the Brahmins chant the magic words, and all harms are healed. How could it be otherwise? For this is a book about success, a book about how to succeed in ritual without really trying, how to win friends and influence gods. It is an advertisement for the Vedic ritual, a before-and-after story of the ninety-pound weakling who wins strength and power by learning how to do it. This being the underlying bias of the text, any tragic or pessimistic elements in the folklore on which it draws will be muted, excised, or transformed. Despite this bias, however, the sharp eyes of the *Jaiminīya* author see, along the twisting path that leads inevitably to the happy ending, a world hedged with dangers at every step—a world full of hatred and rivalry, destructive passions and deceptive bargains, threatening fathers and challenging sons, insatiable demonesses and promiscuous wives. The great force of these dangers makes the proper use of the ritual all the more crucial, all the more difficult, and all the more wonderful.

7
Conclusion: Why Is This Brāhmaṇa Different from All Other Brāhmaṇas?

The same attitude that led the early European Indologists to assume that the Brāhmaṇas were devoid of inspiration led them to assume that they were devoid of individuality. As Max Müller put it, "There are old and new Brāhmaṇas, but the most modern hardly differ in style and language from the most ancient" (Müller 1860, p. 435). This statement can claim a truth status hardly higher than the old racist cliché (by no means unrelated to Max Müller's assertion) that all Chinese look alike. Granted, we cannot prove that any Brāhmaṇa was composed by a single author. But not only do the Brāhmaṇas constitute distinct schools of thought; within those schools there are highly significant variations. When we look at the *Jaiminīya* myths one by one and compare them not only with the other texts of the period but with their narrative ancestors and descendants, we see countless points of essential difference. These points form clusters that we can identify as typical of the *Jaiminīya*.

The first point is that the *Jaiminīya* tells stories. It tells more stories, longer stories, and better stories than any other Brāhmaṇa. It tells stories for the sake of stories, *ars gratia artis*; it tells the Vedic equivalent of shaggy-dog stories. This point was noted implicitly even by Oertel, Caland, and Whitney; it is the first and most striking idiosyncrasy of the

Jaiminīya. Second, these stories form certain patterns. They are pitched on a modest plane of existence, human rather than cosmic; they are banal, everyday, and ordinary in both their settings and their concerns but not in what they say about those settings or in the way they express those concerns. They are also passionate and vivid in their descriptions of events and in the symbolism they use to express those events; they are violent, colorful, lavish in animal images and body symbolism, extravagant in their depiction of human emotions. The stories are also very funny. They are particularly rich in the use of startling colloquialisms, which are all the more striking when set in a formal context. They are frequently highly obscene—not merely erotic, or redolent of fertility, but downright obscene. They seem to glory in extreme forms of sexual behavior and often depict these activities as highly dangerous. They tell many stories about women, and they often use a female image to replace the male image that appears in a parallel text.

What are we to make of this syndrome? Many of these characteristics are typical of folktales the world over, though they are more common in some cultures than in others. To say that these qualities characterize the *Jaiminīya vis-à-vis* other Brāhmaṇas, therefore, is merely to say that the *Jaiminīya* author was a folklorist. It might also be said, however, that these lusty concerns were dear to the heart of the *Jaiminīya* author and that he expressed them not by fabricating his own stories and introducing them into the text but by dragging in the old stories that he knew and loved—loved because they expressed the meanings that he saw in life as well as in the texts. Why didn't he make up his own stories? It was not, I think, for any lack of "overpowering imagination," as Oertel sneered, for surely no one could have told the stories so well, and in such delightful detail, had he lacked imagination. It was rather because, in ancient India, an artist had a very limited amount of room in which to stretch his limbs. It is, after all, quite amazing that the *Jaiminīya* diverged as far as it did from the usual ways of commenting on a Vedic sacrifice; perhaps it was permissible to throw in a story here or there as long as it was a *traditional* story. Or perhaps he used these stories simply because he could not imagine any better ones, because they were just the best stories he knew.

How can we disentangle the meaning of the tales in the *Jaiminīya* (a meaning which must include the private meanings of the author) from the meaning of the tales on which he based his own versions (a meaning which must include the private meanings of previous Indian authors)? We can't, of course; but we can discern a difference in emphasis, perhaps, or a difference in tone or implication. I know no better discussion of this delicate balance than David Grene's remarks on Homer:

> The poet of the *Odyssey* is deeply and consciously concerned with the nature of the poet in relation to the raw material of his poetry, which are the epic stories. These stories must have had overtones of meaning that contradicted his own vision. Which means that the poem he composed presents its truth in an almost but not quite self-conscious relation to an older world, now outmoded, the reality of which at any time is toyed with, doubted, held in suspense and then in this ambiguous light made the substance of his created world of illusion. It is with this peculiar truth, bred of conscious contrast with something else and original in its new infusion of meaning, that I propose to deal. [Grene 1969b, p. 50]

The difficulties that hedge this enterprise—primarily the absence of versions of the epics older than Homer's own—are also present, to some degree, when we try to apply this approach to the *Jaiminīya*, though we do have occasional scraps of the *Ṛg Veda* and other Brāhmaṇas against which to measure the art of the *Jaiminīya*. But the rewards are equally present: the possibility of catching a glimpse of a poet appropriating to himself the particular pieces of an inherited tradition that speak to him; for this is something that all of us do, with greater or lesser success, whenever we confront one of our own classics.

But what distinguishes the *Jaiminīya* stories from other Brāhmaṇas is not merely the element of folklore, for the *Jaiminīya* stories differ from folktales, even other Indian folktales, in several significant respects. Perhaps most striking to a Western audience is the degree to which the *Jaiminīya* expresses sexual violence in an unmasked form; things that are latent, symbolized by other things, in the West are manifest, symbolized only by themselves, in this text. Where Western texts would use blinding or beheading (which also occur in Indian texts) to symbolize castration, Kutsa actually ties down his father's balls. Or so it seems.

When is a phallus not a phallus? When it is a phallic symbol. This was a bone of contention between Freud and Jung for many years. As Jung wrote,

> Unfortunately, Freud's idea of sexuality is incredibly elastic and so vague that it can be made to include almost anything. . . . Take, for instance, the so-called phallic symbols which are supposed to stand for the *membrum virile* and nothing more. Psychologically speaking, the *membrum* is itself . . . an emblem of something whose wider content is not at all easy to determine . . . . [Jung 1974, p. 105]

But the nonsymbolic aspects of symbols continued to bedevil psychoanalysts:

> As somebody (Bernfeld?) once remarked, an aeroplane is a symbol of erection, and the fact that one can also use it for going from Paris to Berlin is merely incidental. [Róheim 1970, p. 156]

These unsymbols (as Prakash Desai has termed the Indian equivalents) present problems for a theory of symbolism like that of psychoanalysis, in which it is assumed that *something* must always be suppressed, censored. If, as Adler is said to have remarked, everything is a symbol of intercourse except intercourse, what is intercourse a symbol of? And does this pose the same sort of problem for Indian mythology that it poses for Western psychoanalysis? In our culture, as Freud rightly pointed out, sex is masked by other symbols; but in India, where sexual symbolism is so transparent, it may be that what is obscene is something else—something else that is symbolized by a simple, everyday thing like a phallus (O'Flaherty 1980a, pp. 86–87). It might be something like death, or God. In "unpacking" the symbolic image, one must beware of taking theology too seriously; but one must also beware of taking sexuality too seriously.

The ease with which symbols vibrate between the theological and the sexual was delightfully demonstrated in the context of a Tantric Indian ritual that a Hindu psychoanalyst (Sudhir Kakar) was attempting to understand:

> In my own conversations with tantriks, I sometimes had the impression that they deliberately (and mischievously) used the multivalence of tantrik terminology to befuddle the perhaps too-earnest outsider. Whenever the term *ānanda* came up in a text . . . and I translated it as "supreme bliss," I was told to forget all the mystical balderdash since *ānanda* was the pure and simple pleasure of intercourse. If I took the concrete meaning, . . . then I was invariably chided for my literal-mindedness since the word in that particular context just happened to stand for "enlightenment." [Kakar 1982, pp. 156–57]

If we apply the cautionary note of this incident to our attempt to analyze the symbolism of the *Jaiminīya*, we may pause in our headlong assumption that gods are symbols of fathers, that the fear of death masks the fear of sex. For if the texts tell us so candidly of their fears of fathers' phalluses and the devouring vaginas of women, what are they hiding? Perhaps they are not hiding *anything*. Perhaps they are hiding the fear that we know underlies the entire sacrificial and textual structure of the Brāhmaṇas: the fear of death. Perhaps we will never know what things they find more frightening than the things that frighten us, what things make them pretend to be frightened by what *really* frightens us.

One final, and highly speculative, answer might be given to the question, "Why is this Brāhmaṇa different from all other

Brāhmaṇas?": "Because it is not different from the *Ṛg Veda* and the *Mahābhārata*." This may seem a trick answer or a riddling answer (such as abound in folktales), but it is a serious assertion. The qualities that cluster in the *Jaiminīya*, in distinction from other Brāhmaṇas—its bawdiness, earthiness, and so forth—characterize the world-view of the *Ṛg Veda*, in contrast with, say, classical Sanskrit literature or even Purāṇic literature. They also characterize the *Mahābhārata*. Again, this may simply indicate that the *Ṛg Veda* and the *Mahābhārata*, like the *Jaiminīya*, incorporate a great deal of folklore. But it may also indicate something a bit more specific.

Many of the tales that can be traced back to the *Ṛg Veda* appear there only *in nuce*; they reappear, greatly expanded and with all the blanks filled in, in the *Mahābhārata*. Scholars have questioned the vitality of the unbroken tradition, the *parampara*, and have hesitated to accept the *Mahābhārata* stories as valid glosses of the Ṛg Vedic allusions, in part because of the great gulf of years that yawns between them (stretching from approximately 1200 B.C. to at least 300 B.C. but probably later) and in part because of the discontinuity between the priestly, sacrificial tradition of the *Ṛg Veda* (where every word was memorized) and the bardic, courtly tradition of the *Mahābhārata* (where the poet could retell the story in his own words). Now, many of the stories mentioned in the *Ṛg Veda* are told in great detail in the *Jaiminīya*; and many of these are retold, in much the same detail, in the *Mahābhārata* (see Appendix 1, part B). It seems possible that the *Jaiminīya*, combining as it does the priestly and the folk traditions, the sacred and the profane, and coming as it does almost precisely halfway between the Vedic and the Epic recensions, provided a kind of stepping-stone, a halfway house for the folk tradition to touch down for a moment in the Sanskrit world before leaping back into the vernacular culture that had always sustained it and would continue to do so for many centuries. Indeed, it is equally possible that the *Jaiminīya* author (or authors) did in fact invent many of the particular images and turns of phrase that make the *Jaiminīya* story different from all the others and that these bright moments then fed back into the folk tradition, enriching it in turn. For every story has to be told for the first time *some*time; every story is an original story, though every version of it may not be equally original.

When we read much of the *Jaiminīya*, we have the feeling that the form is familiar but that the story is new. The peculiarity of the *Jaiminīya* version of the tale may reflect, on some deep level, its individual perception of danger, despite the mandatory veneer of sacrificial safety. As Tolstoy pointed out, all happy families are alike, but each unhappy family is unhappy in its own way. The sacrificial success story—the happy family—is alike in all Brāhmaṇas, but the haunting misgivings—the unhappy families, in which fathers kill sons and women devour their husbands—are different in each individual Brāhmaṇa and most distinctively so in the *Jaiminīya*. The shadows that are preserved in the *Jaiminīya* stories are different from the shadows cast, in the *Ṛg Veda* and in the *Mahābhārata*, by the same towering fears that loom over the human imagination.

Appendix 1

A List of the *Jaiminīya Brāhmaṇa* Stories Translated in This Work

with Names of Sanskrit Chants and Variants in Other Vedic Texts and in the *Mahābhārata*

I list the *Jaiminīya* stories in the order in which they appear in the original text, followed by the Sanskrit name of the chant to which the story is related; I then list (A) variants of the story in other Vedic texts and (B) variants of the story in the *Mahābhārata*.

1\. 42–44 "Bhṛgu's Journey in the Other World" (*Agnihotram*)
- (A) *ŚPB* 11. 6. 1. 1–13. Cf. *RV* 10. 135; *KU* 1–6; *TB* 3. 11. 8. 1–6
- (B) *MBh* 13. 70–71: Nāciketa, cursed by his father, goes to Yama
  MBh 1. 3. 145–75: Uttanka goes to the underworld and views symbolic scenes
  MBh 13. 117. 34: *Lex talionis*: be eaten in the other world

1\. 97–98 "The Gods Make Men Evil"
- (A) *JB* 3. 72
- (B) *MBh* 13. 40. 3–10: The jealous gods use women to make men evil

1\. 125–27 "The Wife of the Gandharva of the Waters" (*Auśanam*)

(A) *JB* 1. 166; *RV* 7. 88. 3–4; *PB* 7. 5. 20: *BŚS* 18. 46; *AB* 3. 21–22

1. 151 "The Sick Boy in the Ditch" (*Paurumīḍham dakṣoṇidhanam*)
(A) *JB* 3. 139; *JB* 1. 171

1. 154–55 "The Gandharva in the Middle" (*Aiḷam*)
(B) *MBh* 12. 329: The treachery of Uśanas

1. 161–63 "Long-Tongue the Demoness" (*Saumitram*)
(A) *RV* 6. 46. 3; *RV* 8. 19. 32; *PB* 13. 6. 9–10; *PB* 12. 11; *AB* 2. 22. 10; *MS* 3. 10. 6; *KāṭhB* 29. 1; *KB* 23. 4; *AV* 7. 38. 3; Sāyaṇa on *RV* 1. 97, *RV* 6. 43. 3, and *AB* 2. 22; scholiast to Pāṇini 4. 1. 59 (cited in Oertel 1897, p. 226)

1. 184 "Trita and His Brothers" (*Traitam*)
(A) Sāyaṇa on *RV* 1. 105 (cited in Oertel 1897, pp. 18–19, and in *Lost Brāhmaṇas,* pp. 19–21)
(B) *MBh* 9. 35: Trita and his brothers

1. 228 "Kutsa Straps Down Indra's Balls" (*Kautsam*)
(A) *RV* 10. 38. 5; *PB* 9. 2. 22; *ŚB* (cited in *Lost Brāhmaṇas,* pp. 63–64); Sāyaṇa on *RV* 10. 38. 5, citing *Chāndogya Brāhmaṇa*
(B) *MBh* 5. 7. 2–35: Arjuna chooses Kṛṣṇa's "self," and Duryodhana chooses armies

2. 126 "The Mortal's Wife and the Dangerous Sacrifice" (*Ekatrikam*)

2. 160–61 "The Son Who Was Better Than His Father" (*Ṛtapeya*)

(A) *JB* 1. 18; *JB* 1. 50

2. 182–83 "How Men Changed Skins with Animals"

2. 269–72 "The Brahmin's Wife with Hair on the Soles of Her Feet" (*Prajāpatinyangam*)
(B) *MBh* 3. 137. 1–20: Yavakrīt

2. 392 "Vasiṣṭha's Dying Son and the Half-Verse" (*RV*)
(A) *JB* 1. 150; *JB* 3. 23; *JB* 3. 26; *JB* 3. 83; *JB* 3. 149; *JB* 3. 204; *PB* 8. 2. 3–4; *PB* 19. 3. 8; *PB* 4. 7. 3; *PB* 4. 21. 11; *TS* 7. 4. 7. 1; *KB* 4. 8; *RV* 7. 32. 36; *Bṛhaddevatā* 6. 28–34; *Bṛhaddevatā* 4. 112–14; Sāyaṇa on *RV* 7. 32; *ŚB* (cited by Venkaṭamādhava in *Lost Brāhmaṇas*, pp. 49–50)
(B) *MBh* 1. 166–68: Vasiṣṭha's son, Śakti.

2. 440–42 "The Divine Bitch" (*RV*)
(A) *RV* 10. 108; *Bṛhaddevatā* 8. 24–36a; *ŚB* (cited by Sāyaṇa on *RV* 1. 62. 3 and in *Lost Brāhmaṇas,* pp. 49–50)
(B) *MBh* 1. 3. 1–10: Saramā and her sons
MBh 13. 40. 39: Indra as a defiling dog

3. 72–74 "The Lover of the Demon's Daughter" (*Nābhakam* and *Traiśokam*)
(A) *ŚB* (cited in *Lost Brāhmaṇas,* pp. 36–38); Sāyaṇa on *RV* 1. 117. 8; Venkaṭamādhava on *RV* 1. 117. 18 and 10. 61. 12
(B) *MBh* 1. 71–72: Uśanas's daughter, Jayantī, and Bṛhaspati's son, Kaca

3. 94–96 "The Charioteer and the Vanishing Fire" (*Vārśam*)

(A) *RV* 5. 2. 1–2; *PB* 13. 3. 12; *Bṛhaddevatā* 5. 14–22; *ŚB* (cited by Sāyaṇa and Venkaṭamādhava on *RV* 5. 2 in *Lost Brāhmaṇas,* pp. 42–43)
(B) *MBh* 1. 5–7: Fire vanishes, wrongly cursed for failing to prevent a rape

3. 120–29 "The Rejuvenation of Cyavana" (*Cyāvanam*)
(A) *JB* 3. 64; *PB* 14. 6. 10; *ŚPB* 4. 1. 5. 1–12
(B) *MBh* 3. 124–25: Cyavana (See also *MBh* 1. 76–80: Yayāti)

3. 159–61 "Vidanvan and the Demon of Intoxication" (*Vaidanvatāni*)
(A) *PB* 13. 11. 10; *ŚPB* 3. 6. 2. 26; *ŚB* (cited by Venkaṭamādhava on *RV* 1. 116. 10 in *Lost Brāhmaṇas,* pp. 25–29)
(B) *MBh* 3. 124–25: Cyavana and the Demon of Intoxication

3. 193–94 "Indra and the Dolphin" (*Śārkaram*)
(A) *PB* 14. 4. 15

3. 197 "The Girl on the Island" (*Jarābodīyam*)
(A) *JB* 3. 18; *PB* 11. 5. 14; *PB* 25. 7. 2

3. 199–200 "Kutsa Seduces Indra's Wife" (*Sauśravasam*)
(A) *RV* 4. 16. 10; *RV* 10. 49. 3–7; Sāyaṇa on *RV* 4. 16. 10
(B) *MBh* 1. 8–11: Ruru gives half of his life to his wife

3. 200–202 "Indra Revives the Son of Kutsa's Enemy" (*Sauśravasam*)
(A) *PB* 14. 6. 8

3. 221 "The Uncle Who Tried to Murder the New-

born Child" (*Vaiyaśvam*)
(B) *MBh* 3. 126. 1–26: Indra nurses Māndhātṛ

3. 234–36 "Indra as the Ram of Medhātithi" (*Maidhātitham*)
(A) *JB* 2. 79–80; *RV* 8. 2. 40; *RV* 8. 8. 20; *PB* 15. 10. 11; *PB* 14. 66. 6; *ŚB* and Veṅkaṭamādhava on *RV* 1. 51. 1 (cited in *Lost Brāhmaṇas*, pp. 5–6)

3. 245–48 "Indra Dances for Upamā" (*Adārasṛt, Bhāradhvajasya*)

3. 270–71 "How Not to Get to Heaven" (*Āsitam*)
(A) *JB* 3. 76; *PB* 12. 11. 9–12

JUB 3. 6.1–3 "The Ghost of the Beloved Uncle" (*Aśarīram*)

Appendix 2
Secondary Literature on Each *Jaiminīya Brāhmaṇa* Story in This Work

1. 42–44	"Bhṛgu's Journey in the Other World" Bodewitz 1973, pp. 99–109; Oertel 1893, pp. 234–38; Oertel 1905a, p. 196; Oertel 1908, p. 123; Lévi 1966, p. 114; Lommel 1950, pp. 53–109; Weber 1855, pp. 237–45; O'Flaherty 1980a, pp. 21–22; O'Flaherty 1984, pp. 90–91
1. 97–98	"The Gods Make Men Evil" Caland 1919, pp. 19–21; O'Flaherty 1976, p. 249
1. 125–27	"The Wife of the Gandharva of the Waters" Oertel 1897, pp. 82–83; Oertel 1907, pp. 82–98; Caland 1931, p. 145; Geldner 1889, pp. 166–68; Pischel 1889, pp. 195–97
1. 151	"The Sick Boy in the Ditch" Caland 1919, pp. 50–51; Oertel 1897, pp. 39–40
1. 154–55	"The Gandharva in the Middle" Caland 1919, pp. 52–53; O'Flaherty 1976, pp. 118–27; O'Flaherty 1975, pp. 289–300
1. 161–63	"Long-Tongue the Demoness" Caland 1919, pp. 60–61; Caland 1931, pp. 328–

29; Oertel 1897, pp. 162–63; Oertel 1899; Oertel 1908, p. 118; Oertel 1898, p. 120; O'Flaherty 1980a, pp. 17–33

1. 184 "Trita and His Brothers"
Oertel 1897, pp. 18–19

1. 228 "Kutsa Straps Down Indra's Balls"
Oertel 1897, pp. 32–33; Oertel 1908, pp. 116–17; Geldner 1889, pp. 170–79; Pischel 1889, pp. 196–97; O'Flaherty 1976, pp. 334–35

2. 126 "The Mortal's Wife and the Dangerous Sacrifice"
Caland 1919, pp. 163–64

2. 160–61 "The Son Who Was Better Than His Father"
Caland 1919, pp. 174–77

2. 182–83 "How Men Changed Skins with Animals"
Caland 1919, pp. 177–80

2. 269–72 "The Brahmin's Wife with Hair on the Soles of Her Feet"
Caland 1919, pp. 190–94

2. 392 "Vasiṣṭha's Dying Son and the Half-Verse"
Oertel 1897, pp. 47–48; Ensink 1968, pp. 572–84

2. 440–42 "The Divine Bitch"
Oertel 1898, pp. 97–103; Oertel 1908, p. 124; Aufrecht 1859, pp. 493–99; Bloomfield 1893, pp. 163–74; O'Flaherty 1975, pp. 71–74

3. 72–74 "The Lover of the Demon's Daughter"
Caland 1919, pp. 234–37; Caland 1931, p. 296; O'Flaherty 1976, pp. 115–16; O'Flaherty 1975, pp. 281–87

3. 94–96 "The Charioteer and the Vanishing Fire"
Caland 1919, pp. 239–43; Oertel 1897, pp.

	20–22; Oertel 1908, pp. 113–15; Sieg 1902, pp. 64–76; O'Flaherty 1981, pp. 101–104
3. 120–29	"The Rejuvenation of Cyavana" Caland 1919, pp. 251–57; Oertel 1897, p. 38; Whitney 1883, pp. viii–xii; Hopkins 1905, pp. 1–67; O'Flaherty 1973, pp. 57–64; O'Flaherty 1975, pp. 56–60
3. 159–61	"Vidanvan and the Demon of Intoxication" Hopkins 1905, p. 63; Caland 1931, p. 343; O'Flaherty 1976, pp. 164–65
3. 193–94	"Indra and the Dolphin" Caland 1919, pp. 266–67; Caland 1931, p. 362
3. 197	"The Girl on the Island" Caland 1919, pp. 269–70; Caland 1931, p. 365
3. 199–200	"Kutsa Seduces Indra's Wife" Caland 1919, pp. 270–73; Caland 1931, pp. 368–69
3. 200–202	"Indra Revives the Son of Kutsa's Enemy" Caland 1919, pp. 270–74
3. 221	"The Uncle Who Tried to Murder the New-born Child" Caland 1919, pp. 267–77; Caland 1931, p. 380
3. 234–36	"Indra as the Ram of Medhātithi" Caland 1919, pp. 278–81; Caland 1931, pp. 419–20; Oertel 1895; Oertel 1897, p. 38; Oertel 1905, p. 194
3. 245–48	"Indra Dances for Upamā" Caland 1919, pp. 284–87; Caland 1931, p. 394
3. 270–71	"How Not to Get to Heaven" Caland 1919, pp. 291–93; Caland 1931, pp. 383–84
JUB 3. 6.1–3	"The Ghost of the Beloved Uncle" Oertel 1894, pp. 188–90

Appendix 3
Tale Types and Motifs

This list, based on Stith Thompson's indexes of Tale Types (TT) and Motifs (M), is suggestive rather than complete; it indicates just a few of the possible motifs and types for the central stories, and it does not give multiple citations for motifs that appear in more than one story. The letters and numbers refer to the Stith Thompson system; Tale Types, as titles, are capitalized.

JB 1. 42–44 "Bhṛgu's Journey in the Other World"
TT 369: The Youth on a Quest for His Lost Father
TT 465C: A Journey to the Other World
TT 466*: Journey to Hell
TT 812: The Devil's Riddle
M: H 1252.1.2: Quest to see if father is in heaven or in hell

JB 1. 97–98 "The Gods Make Men Evil"
M: A 185.14.1: God causes mortals' sins

JB 1. 125–27 "The Wife of the Gandharva in the Waters"
TT 461: Three Hairs from the Devil's Beard
TT 812: The Devil's Riddle

M: G 530.1: Help from ogre's wife (mistress)
G 661.2: Ogre's secret overheard by masquerading as bird

JB 1. 154–55 "The Gandharva in the Middle"
M: A 189.1: Mortal as ally of gods

JB 1. 161–63 "Long-Tongue the Demoness"
M: A 164.6: God as lover of giantess
D 457.14.1: Tongue of ogress becomes surfboard
F 582: Poison damsel
F 585.1: Fatal enticements of phantom women
G 229.5: Beautiful witch
G 264: La Belle Dame sans Merci

JB 1. 184 "Trita and His Brothers"
TT 654: The Three Brothers
M: H 934.4: Elder brother imposes task

JB 2. 182–83 "How Men Changed Skins with Animals"
M: A 1715: Animals from transformed men

JB 2. 269–72 "The Brahmin's Wife with Hair on the Soles of Her Feet"
M: G 216: Witch with extraordinary feet
K 1843: Wife deceives husband with substituted bedmate.

JB 2. 440–42 "The Divine Bitch"
M: A 165.2.1: Animals as messengers of the gods
B 182.1.7: Magic bitches enchanted by fairy music
G 211.1.8: Witch in form of dog

JB 3. 72–74 "The Lover of the Demon's Daughter"
TT 313: The Girl as Helper in the Hero's Flight
M: G 530.2: Help from ogre's daughter

JB 3. 94–96 "The Charioteer and the Vanishing Fire"
TT 411A: The King and the Lamia
M: D 439.6: Fire takes the form of a woman and runs away

JB 3. 120–29 "The Rejuvenation of Cyavana"
M: D 1887: Rejuvenation by bathing
H 923.1: Wife rescues husband from supernatural
R 152: Wife rescues husband

JB 3. 159–61 "Vidanvan and the Demon of Intoxication"
M: K 776: Capture by intoxication
K 871: Fatal intoxication

JB 3. 197 "The Girl on the Island"
TT 306A: The Pursuit of the Heavenly Maiden
TT 310: The Maiden in the Tower

JB 3. 199–200 "Kutsa Seduces Indra's Wife"
TT 921: Oedipus
M: T 92.9: Father and son as love rivals
T 412: Mother-son incest

JB 3. 221 "The Uncle Who Tried to Murder the Newborn Child"
M: K 512: Compassionate executioner
M 371.2: Exposure of child to prevent fulfillment of parricide prophecy
R 131: Exposed or abandoned child rescued

T 611.1: Child nourished by sucking its own fingers
T 611.1.1: Child nourished by sucking thumb of a god

JUB 3. 6. 1–3 "The Ghost of the Beloved Uncle"
M: E 327: Dead father's friendly return

Bibliography

Sanskrit Texts and Commentaries

Aitareya Brāhmaṇa. With the commentary of Sāyaṇa. Calcutta, 1896.

Atharva Veda. With the commentary of Sāyaṇa. Bombay, 1895.

Baudhāyana Śrauta Sūtra. Edited by W. Caland. 2 vols. Calcutta, 1904–15.

Bṛhadāraṇyaka Upaniṣad. In *One Hundred and Eight Upanishads*. Bombay, 1913.

Bṛhaddevatā of Śaunaka. Harvard Oriental Series, vol. 5. Cambridge, Mass., 1904.

Gopatha Brāhmaṇa. Leiden, 1919.

Jaiminīya [Talavakara] Brāhmaṇa of the Sāma Veda. Complete text, critically edited for the first time by Raghu Vira and Lokesh Chandra. Sarasvati Vihara Series, vol. 31. Nagpur, 1954.

Jaiminīya [Talavakara] Upaniṣad Brāhmaṇa. Edited by Hanns Oertel. Calcutta, 1921.

Jaiminīyārṣeya and Jaiminīyopaniṣad Brāhmaṇas. Edited by Bellikoth Ramachandra. Kendriya Sanskrit Vidyapeetha Series, vols. 5–6. Tirupathi, 1967.

Kāṭhaka Brāhmaṇa. In *Lost Brāhmaṇas*.

Kauṣītaki Brāhmaṇa. Wiesbaden, 1968.

Kaṭha Upaniṣad. In *One Hundred and Eight Upanishads*. Bombay, 1913.

Mahābhārata. Critical edition. Poona, 1933–69.

Maitrāyaṇī Saṃhitā. Edited by L. von Schroeder. Wiesbaden, 1881.

Manu (*Mānavadharmaśāstra*). With the commentary of Medhātithi. Calcutta, 1932.

Pañcaviṃśa [Tāṇḍya-mahā-] Brāhmaṇa. With the commentary of Sāyaṇa. Calcutta 1869–74.

Ṛg Veda. With the commentary of Sāyaṇa. 6 vols. London, 1890–92.

Ṣaḍviṃśa Brāhmaṇa. With the commentary of Sāyaṇa. Edited by Bellikoth Ramachandra Sharma. Kendriya Sanskrit Vidyapeetha Series, vol. 9. Tirupathi, 1967.

Śāṭyāyaṇa Brāhmaṇa. Known only from fragments. Cited in *Lost Brāhmaṇas*.

Śāṅkhāyana Brāhmaṇa. Edited by Harinarayan Bhattacharya. Calcutta, 1970.

Śatapatha Brāhmaṇa. Edited by A. Weber. Calcutta, 1903.

Taittirīya Brāhmaṇa. With the commentary of Sāyaṇa. Calcutta, 1859.

Taittirīya Saṃhitā. With the commentary of Mādhava. Calcutta, 1860.

Vājasaneyi Saṃhitā. Berlin, 1952.

Venkaṭamādhava. Commentary on the *Ṛg Veda*. Known in fragments. Cited in *Lost Brāhmaṇas*.

NOTE: Fragments from several lost Brāhmaṇas, notably the *Śāṭyāyaṇa*, and from several lost commentaries, notably that of Venkaṭamādhava, are collected in Batakrishna Ghosh's *Collection of the Fragments of Lost Brāhmaṇas*. Bharatiya Mahavidyalaya Vedic Series no. 1. Calcutta, 1947.

Translations and Studies in European Languages

Aarne, Antti, and Thompson, Stith. 1961. *The Types of the Folktale*. Helsinki.

Aufrecht, Theodor. 1859. "Saramā's Botschaft." *Zeitschrift der Deutschen Morgenländischen Gesellschaft* 13:493–99.

Bloomfield, Maurice. 1893. "The Two Dogs of Yama." *JAOS* 15:163–73.

Bodewitz, H. W. 1973. *Jaiminīya Brāhmaṇa I, 1–65, Translation and Commentary, with a Study of the Agnihotra and Prāṇāgnihotra*. Leiden.
Brown, W. Norman. 1928. *The Indian and Christian Miracles of Walking on the Water*. Chicago and London.
Burnell, A. C. 1878. "A Legend from the *Talavakara* (or *Jaiminīya*) *Brāhmaṇa* of the *Sāma Veda*." *Indian Antiquary* 13:16–29. Also printed in *Atti del IV Congresso Internationale degli Orientalisti (Firenze)* 20 (1878):97–111.
Caland, W. 1907. *Die Jaiminīya Saṃhitā, mit einer Einleitung über die Sāmavedaliteratur*. Indische Forschungen, vol. 2. Breslau.
———. 1915. "Over en Uit het Jaiminīya Brāhmaṇa." *Verslagen en medeelingen der Koninklijke Akademie van Wetenschappen, Amsterdam* 51:1–21.
———. 1919. *Das Jaiminīya Brāhmaṇa in Auswahl: Text, Übersetzung, Indices*. Amsterdam.
———. 1931. *Pañcaviṃśa Brāhmaṇa: The Brāhmaṇa of Twenty-Five Chapters*. Translated by W. Caland. Calcutta, 1931.
Coomaraswamy, A. K. 1956. *Christian and Oriental Philosophy of Art*. New York.
Deppert, Joachim. 1977. *Rudras Geburt: Systematische Untersuchungen zum Inzest in der Mythologie der Brāhmaṇas*. Wiesbaden.
Eggeling, Julius. 1882. *The Śatapatha Brāhmaṇa, according to the Text of the Mādhyandina School*. Translated by Julius Eggeling. 5 vols. Oxford.
Ensink, J. 1968. "Mitrasaha, Sudāsa's Son, with the Spotted Feet." Pp. 573–84 in *Pratidānam: Indian, Iranian, and Indo-European Studies Presented to Franciscus Bernardus Jacobus Kuiper on his Sixtieth Birthday*. Edited by J. C. Heesterman et al. The Hague.
Farquhar, J. N. 1920. *An Outline of the Religious Literature of India*. Oxford.
Geldner, K. F. 1889. "Prapitvā." Pp. 155–79 in vol. 2 of *Vedische Studien*, edited by K. F. Geldner and Richard Pischel. 3 vols. Stuttgart.
Grene, David. 1969a. *Reality and the Heroic Pattern*. Chicago.

———. 1969b. "The Odyssey: An Approach." *Midway* 9:47–68.

Hopkins, E. W. 1905. "The Fountain of Youth." *JAOS* 26:1–67.

———. 1909. "Gods and Saints of the Great Brāhmaṇa." *Transactions of the Connecticut Academy of Arts and Sciences* 15:19–69.

Jung, C. G. 1974. *Dreams*. Translated by R. F. C. Hull. Princeton.

Kakar, Sudhir. 1978. *The Inner World: A Psycho-Analytic Study of Childhood and Society in India*. Oxford.

———. 1982. *Shamans, Mystics, and Doctors*. New York.

Lanman, Charles. 1884. *Sanskrit Reader*. Cambridge, Mass.

Lévi, Sylvain. 1966. *La doctrine du sacrifice dans les Brāhmaṇas*. Paris.

Lommel, Herman. 1950. "Bhrigu im Jenseits." *Paideuma* 4:93–109.

Macdonell, Arthur A. 1900. *A History of Sanskrit Literature*. New York.

Müller, F. Max. 1860. *A History of Ancient Sanskrit Literature*. 2d ed. London.

———. 1900. *Chips from a German Workshop*. Vol. 1. New York.

Nandy, Ashis. 1980. *Alternative Sciences*. Delhi.

Obeyesekere, Gananath. 1980. "The Rebirth Eschatology and Its Transformations: A Contribution to the Sociology of Early Buddhism." Pp. 137–64 in *Karma and Rebirth in Classical Indian Traditions*, edited by Wendy Doniger O'Flaherty. Berkeley and Los Angeles.

———. 1981. *Medusa's Hair: An Essay on Personal Symbols and Religious Experience*. Chicago.

Oertel, H. 1893. "Extracts from the *Jaiminīya Brāhmaṇa* and *Upaniṣad-Brāhmaṇa*." *JAOS* 15:233–51.

———. 1894. "The *Jaiminīya* or *Talavakāra Upaniṣad Brāhmaṇa*: Text, Translation, and Notes." *JAOS* 16.1:79–260.

———. 1895. "The Legend of Indra's Visit to Medhātithi." *JAOS* 16:ccxl–xli.

———. 1897. "Contributions from the *Jaiminīya*

Brāhmaṇa to the History of the Brāhmaṇa Literature, First Series." *JAOS* 18:15–48.
———. 1898. "Contributions . . ., Second Series." *JAOS* 19:97–125.
———. 1899. "The Jaiminīya Brāhmaṇa Version of the Dīrghajihvī Legend." *Actes du Onzième Congrès International des Orientalistes, Paris 1897*, vol. 1, pp. 225–39. Paris.
———. 1902. "Contributions . . . Fourth Series." *JAOS* 23:325–49.
———. 1905a. "Contributions . . . Fifth Series." *JAOS* 26:176–196.
———. 1905b. "Additions to the Fifth Series of Contributions. . . ." *JAOS* 26:306–14.
———. 1907. "Contributions . . . Sixth Series." *JAOS* 28:81–98.
———. 1909. "Contributions . . . Seventh Series." *Transactions of the Connecticut Academy of Arts and Sciences* 15:155–98.
———. 1908. "Altindische Parallelen zu abendländischen Erzählungsmotiven." Pp. 113–24 in *Studien zur vergleichenden Literaturgeschichte*, vol. 8, edited by Max Koch. Berlin.
O'Flaherty, Wendy Doniger. 1973. *Asceticism and Eroticism in the Mythology of Śiva*. Oxford.
———. 1975. *Hindu Myths*. Harmondsworth.
———. 1976. *The Origins of Evil in Hindu Mythology*. Berkeley and Los Angeles.
———. 1980a. *Women, Androgynes, and Other Mythical Beasts*. Chicago.
———. 1980b. *Karma and Rebirth in Classical Indian Traditions*. Berkeley and Los Angeles.
———. 1981. *The Rig Veda: An Anthology*. Harmondsworth.
———. 1984. *Dreams, Illusion, and Other Realities*. Chicago.
Parpola, A. 1973. *The Literature and Study of the Jaiminīya Sāmaveda*. Helsinki.
Pischel, Richard. 1889. "Ātka." Pp. 193–204, in vol. 2 of *Vedische Studien*, edited by K. F. Geldner and Richard Pischel. 3 vols. Stuttgart.

Ramanujan, A. K. 1972. "The Indian Oedipus." Pp. 127–37 in *Indian Literature: Proceedings of a Seminar*, edited by Arabinda Podder. Simla.

———. 1981. "Is There an Indian Way of Thinking?" Typescript.

Róheim, Géza. 1970. "Telepathy in a Dream." Pp. 147–57 in *Psychoanalysis and the Occult*, edited by George Devereux. New York.

Rycroft, Charles. 1979. *The Innocence of Dreams*. New York.

Sieg, Emil. 1902. *Die Sagenstoffe des Ṛgveda und die indische Itihāsatradition*. Berlin.

Smith, Brian K. 1984. *Ritual, Resemblance, and Hierarchy: The Case of the Vedic Sacrifice*. Ph. D. dissertation, University of Chicago.

Smith, Jonathan Z. 1982. "The Bare Facts of Ritual." Pp. 53–65 in *Imagining Religion*. Chicago.

Staal, Frits. 1979. "The Meaninglessness of Ritual." *Numen* 26:1–18.

Thompson, Stith. 1955–58. *Motif-Index of Folk Literature*. 6 vols. Bloomington, Indiana.

——— and Aarne, Antti. 1964. *See* Aarne.

——— and Balys, Jonas. 1958. *The Oral Tales of India*. Bloomington, Indiana.

——— and Roberts, Warren E. 1960. *Types of Indic Oral Tales*. Helsinki.

Weber, A. 1855. "Eine Legende des *Śatapatha Brāhmaṇa* über die strafende Vergeltung nach dem Tode." *Zeitschrift der Deutschen Morgenländischen Gesellschaft* 9:273–89.

Whitney, W. D. 1873. *Oriental and Linguistic Studies*. New York.

———. 1882. "Eggeling's Translation of the *Çatapatha Brāhmaṇa*." *American Journal of Philology* 3:391–98.

———. 1883. "On the *Jaiminīya* or *Talavakara Brāhmaṇa*." *JAOS* 5:viii–xii.

———. 1892. "On the Narrative Use of Imperfect and Perfect in the Brāhmaṇas." *Transactions of the American Philological Association* 23:5–34.

Index